'Niall, what p[art] not understa[nd?]'

The coolness of S[affron's] tone got through to him, and she saw a dark scowl cross his face.

'The word "no" I understand perfectly,' he declared harshly. 'What I can't get my head round is why you're using it when you don't really mean it.'

Then, as she gasped in shock and fury at the arrogance of his words, he shrugged his broad shoulders dismissively and shook his dark head.

'But you did, and so I'll just have to accept that you obviously don't know your own mind as well as I do mine. All right, Saffron— I can wait.'

Kate Walker was born in Nottinghamshire but as she grew up in Yorkshire she has always felt that her roots were there. She met her husband at university and she originally worked as a children's librarian but after the birth of her son she returned to her old childhood love of writing. When she's not working, she divides her time between her family, their three cats, and her interests of embroidery, antiques, film and theatre, and, of course, reading.

Recent titles by the same author:

CALYPSO'S ENCHANTMENT

NO HOLDING BACK

BY
KATE WALKER

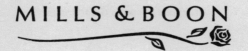

MILLS & BOON

*MILLS & BOON and the Rose Device
are trademarks of the publisher.
Harlequin Mills & Boon Limited,
Eton House, 18-24 Paradise Road, Richmond, Surrey TW9 1SR
This edition published by arrangement with
Harlequin Enterprises B.V.*

© Kate Walker 1995

ISBN 0 263 79269 2

*Set in Times Roman 10 on 11½ pt.
01-9511-54870 C1*

Made and printed in Great Britain

CHAPTER ONE

SAFFRON pushed open the office door and sighed with relief when she saw that the room beyond was empty. Having come this far, she didn't want to be put off by the sight of Owen's elegant secretary, and she didn't know what explanation she could have given that would have persuaded Stella not to buzz through to her employer to let him know that she was there. Everything would be spoiled if he had any warning of her presence.

And she didn't want to risk the possibility that she might lose the impetus that had driven her so far, the wonderful, liberating rush of anger that had pushed away any thought of doubt or hesitation. She had nurtured that feeling ever since last night, since the moment it had become obvious that Owen was not going to turn up. Then, her mood had been so bad that simply recalling it now brought a red haze of fury up before her eyes, pushing her into action as, without bothering to knock, she flung open the door and marched into the office beyond.

'You'll know why I'm here!'

The man seated at the desk had his dark head bent, his attention directed at some notes that he was making on a pad in front of him, but Saffron barely spared him a glance. She wouldn't have been able to see him too clearly anyway, that mist of anger blurring her vision so that he was just a dark, indecipherable shape. Her fingers shaking with the intensity of her feelings, she tugged at the buttons on her coat, vaguely aware of the fact that, surprised by her appearance, he had glanced up sharply.

'You promised me a special night out——'

Her voice wasn't pitched the way she had wanted it to be, pent up emotions making it too high and tight.

'"A special night for a special girl", you said! I waited for you for over three hours——'

That was better. Now she sounded more confident, stronger altogether, the sort of woman people would take notice of.

'But you couldn't even be bothered to phone—to explain. Well, that's your hard luck!'

She certainly had his attention now. His stillness, the way he sat upright, his hand still gripping the pen, told her that. But she couldn't look him straight in the face or she would lose her nerve. The last button on her coat came undone and she drew a deep, gasping breath.

'I just thought I'd let you know that *this* is what you turned down——'

As she spoke, she flung open the trenchcoat, revealing the skimpy scarlet silk basque, laced up the front in black, the matching provocatively small panties and the delicate, lacy web of a suspender belt that supported the sheerest of stockings on her long, slender legs which tapered down to bright scarlet leather sandals, their spiky heels giving her five feet eight a further impressive three inches.

In the stunned silence that followed her dramatic gesture, Saffron finally found that her eyes would focus at last, and she turned a half defiant, half teasing look on the man at the desk. Only to recoil in shocked horror as her eyes met the contemptuous, coolly assessing stare of a pair of light grey eyes—eyes that in their silvery paleness bore no resemblance to the bright blue gaze she had expected to see.

This wasn't Owen! She had never even seen this man before in her life!

Frozen into panic-stricken immobility, Saffron could only watch, transfixed, her own brown eyes wide and shocked, as that narrow-eyed gaze slid slowly, deliberately downwards from her hotly burning cheeks. They lingered appreciatively on the amount of creamy flesh, the soft curves of her breasts exposed and enhanced by the ridiculous slivers of material, and on her dark hair, falling in wanton disarray around the pale skin of her shoulders.

'Very nice,' he said at last, his voice a smooth drawl, making Saffron think wildly of rich, dark honey oozing slowly over gravel. 'Very nice, indeed. But, believe me, if I *had* been offered something so very tempting, then in no circumstances would I have been fool enough to turn it down.'

The mocking humour that threaded through that low, attractive voice was blended together with a warmly sensual note of appreciation, breaking into the trance-like state that had held Saffron frozen.

'Why, you——!' Words failed her, shock and disbelief forming a knot in her throat that threatened to choke her.

'Oh, come on, honey——' His smile was as slow and provocative as his voice. 'If you don't want the customers to be interested then you shouldn't display the goods quite so attractively.'

'Display—customers!' Saffron exploded as the insulting implications of that taunt sank in. 'I don't want you——'

'No?' The amusement in the single syllable stung more than any harsher comment might have.

'No! You're—you're not who I meant—you're the wrong man entirely!'

'Is that so? Well, I hate to disagree with you, but from where I'm sitting I'm the *right* man—and you——'

Those silvery eyes moved over her again, seeming to burn where they rested, so that Saffron's pale skin glowed in fiery embarrassment.

'You're exactly what I've been looking for—so if you'll just tell me your terms, I'm sure we'll be able to come to some arrangement.'

'Terms!' Saffron spluttered, unable to believe that this was happening to her. 'We will do no such thing! We——'

She broke off on a terrified gasp as the man dropped his pen on to the desk and straightened, as if about to get to his feet. The tiny movement shattered what little remained of her self-control, and whirling in panic she headed for the door, running as fast as she could towards the lift.

'Wait! Please——'

The lift doors were just closing as Saffron reached them, but luckily her strangled squawk of near-panic caught the ears of the solitary female occupant, who reacted swiftly, obligingly pressing a firm finger on the 'Door Hold' button, halting them in their tracks. A couple of seconds later, with a metallic rattle, they jerked apart once more, allowing her to step inside.

'Thanks!'

It came out on a choked gasp as, not daring to look behind her, she hurried into the compartment, huddling into the far corner and giving a deep sigh of relief as the doors slid closed again and the lift started to move smoothly downwards. If that man had followed her, then surely she'd got away from him now.

'In a hurry?' The other woman, someone she vaguely remembered from Richards' last Christmas party, enquired smilingly.

'You could say that!' Saffron's response was wry, her voice still shaking in a way that she prayed her companion would believe to be the result of her dash along the corridor and so not ask any awkward questions.

'And those heels aren't made to run in——'

'They most definitely are not!' she returned feelingly. How she wished she could kick them off—her feet were killing her! But she was sure that if she did she would never get the damn things back on again. She had borrowed them from her friend and workmate Kate and, as well as being much higher than anything she normally wore, they were a very tight fit indeed—Kate being built on a much smaller scale than her tall, fine-boned friend.

Saffron pushed a disturbed hand through the tumbled mane of her shining dark brown hair, holding her coat closely fastened with the other, her lips twisting slightly as she recalled the way Kate had described the offending footwear, the words repeating inside her head with a worrying significance.

'They're real tart's shoes,' her friend had said, laughter lifting her voice. But now, remembering, Saffron felt no trace of her earlier amusement. If that was how that man might describe what she was wearing on her feet— then what words would he use to describe *her*?

'Are you all right?' Her companion had noticed her involuntary shudder, and was studying her more closely.

'As a matter of fact, I think I'm going down with flu,' Saffron improvised hastily. 'That's why I'm going home.'

She prayed that the explanation would cover any other betraying reactions she might be showing. She knew that her cheeks were brightly flushed, and that probably her brown eyes were overbright and glittering with reaction to the shock she had just had. The way she was clutching her coat to her must also look peculiar, to say the least, particularly in this well-heated building. That thought had her instinctively tightening her grip on the black trenchcoat. She had reacted automatically, not thinking straight enough to check that all the buttons were fastened, the belt securely tied. If it should gape open, this woman would get the shock of her life.

'Bed's probably the best place for you, then.'

Somehow Saffron managed a vague murmur that might have been agreement, her mind too busy with other, more troublesome matters. Thinking straight! She hadn't been thinking at all, just reacting. All that had been in her head had been the need to get out of there fast, to hide her embarrassment, get away from those coolly mocking eyes, that hateful voice.

It was all Owen's fault, she told herself furiously. If he hadn't stood her up last night, then none of this would have happened. The bad temper that his neglect had sparked off in her had burned all through the night, not at all improved by a restless, unsatisfactory attempt at sleep. The fact that as the morning progressed it had become obvious that Owen wasn't even going to bother to ring up and explain had been positively the last straw, finally causing the simmering volcano of fury inside her to boil up and spill over like red-hot lava.

'I'm not going to put up with this, Kate!' she had declared at last, slamming the phone down on yet another caller whom she had hoped might just be Owen, offering a very belated excuse for his non-appearance, but in fact had turned out to be an assistant at the laundry with a thoroughly mundane enquiry about the number of napkins and tablecloths they had sent in their usual Monday morning bundle of linen. 'He's just taking me for granted, and I won't stand for it.'

'Perhaps he was ill,' Kate had suggested, her tone soothing.

But Saffron had refused to allow herself to be placated.

'How ill do you have to be before you're incapable of using a phone?'

'My, you *have* got your knickers in a twist, haven't you?' Kate teased, studying her friend's indignant face with a touch of amused curiosity. 'This isn't just about being stood up, is it? There's more to it than that. I know you—and I haven't seen you this worked up in a long time.'

'I don't like being taken for granted,' Saffron muttered, not meeting Kate's eyes. She wished the other girl didn't know her quite so well—well enough to put her finger on an uncomfortable spot in her feelings.

'And——?' Kate prompted laughingly, but then the flush of embarrassment that had shaded Saffron's cheeks was replaced by a stronger, hotter colour, that could only be the result of deep embarrassment. 'Saffy!' she exclaimed in frank disbelief. 'You didn't!'

'Didn't what?'

'Don't stall me! You know perfectly well what I mean. You've been fretting over things for weeks, trying to make your mind up. So, confess—had you finally decided that last night was to have been *the* night?'

'I don't want to just drift any more, Kate. I'm ready for some sort of commitment. I want a future—I have been seeing him for over six months.'

'But I never thought you saw him in the light of a grand passion. Poor Owen.' Kate laughed. 'All these months he's been begging you to go to bed with him and getting nowhere, and when you finally decide to let him have his wicked way he doesn't even turn up. No wonder you're hopping mad.'

'You should have seen me last night,' Saffron put in, a touch of rueful amusement mingling with the quiver of anger in her words. 'There I was, all done up like a dog's dinner—little black dress, perfume, stockings and suspenders—the works. I even bought new underwear.' The shake in her voice grew more pronounced.

'Oh, Saffy——'

'It was pure silk!'

Her anger was growing again, fighting against the tenuous grip she had on it. She had felt such a fool, sitting there, dressed up, made-up—keyed up—waiting for a man who didn't come.

Kate's whistle was long and low. 'The sacrificial lamb! It's a pity Owen doesn't know just what he missed! You'll have to find some way of getting that home to him.'

That was when the idea came to her, Saffron reflected as the lift by-passed the second floor. Her anger wouldn't be appeased unless she did something about the way Owen had treated her, and Kate's remark had given her the perfect way to show him how she felt.

'Well, here we are.'

The voice of her companion broke into her thoughts, bringing her back to the present with an abruptness that, combined with the jerky movement of the lift as it came to a halt, almost knocked her off-balance, so that she fell back against the wall.

'Are you OK?'

'Fine——'

It was impossible to concentrate on what she was saying, all her attention directed towards the lift doors as they started to open. Was that man still upstairs in the office, or had he followed her? And if so, having missed the lift, had he come down the staircase after her?

She could just imagine those long legs—for such an impressive torso had to be matched by an equally powerful lower half—taking the stairs two or more at a time, matching or possibly even outstripping the speed of the lift in which she had travelled. So, was he, even now, prowling around the hall, waiting for her? The thought sent a shiver of apprehension sliding down her spine.

A hasty, cautious inspection of the reception area reassured her on that point—temporarily, at least. He wasn't anywhere in sight, but that didn't mean that he wasn't on his way down. He might appear at any moment, so she had better not take any risks. The sooner she was out of here the better.

'How will you get home?'

'I've got my car——'

Saffron was hurrying across the well-worn floor as she spoke, pulling open the door in a rush. A cold wind, touched with a hint of rain, sneaked around her as she stepped outside, making her shiver uncomfortably, painfully aware of how little she had on under the protective layer of the coat. That thought brought a rush of burning colour to her cheeks, something that clearly worried the other woman.

'Are you sure you're fit to drive? Perhaps I should ring upstairs for someone——'

'No!' If he thought she was still in the building, heaven alone knew how he might react. She couldn't face him again; couldn't look him in the eye. 'I'll be all right— honest—it's not very far——'

'Well, if you're positive...'

She still sounded unconvinced, and Saffron had to fight hard not to scream at her in panic as, through the large plate glass doors, she saw the other lift open and a tall, masculine figure appear in the hall, looking round him a way that made her think unnervingly of a hunting tiger. She could almost imagine him scenting the air, breathing in the trace of her perfume...

'I have to go——'

Reacting purely instinctively, she kicked off the crippling shoes—she would buy Kate another pair—and

turned to run towards the spot where her car was parked.
The wind seemed to have found every opening in her
coat, sliding in at the neck, whipping around her hem,
revealing far more than was comfortable to her already
precarious peace of mind, but she was oblivious to the
cold and discomfort of her bare feet on the tarmac,
reaching her small Fiat with a sigh of relief.

It was as she slid into the driving-seat and pushed her
wild, wind-blown dark hair back from her face that she
saw the other car, the one that, blinded by her anger,
she hadn't noticed on her arrival at the factory. Sleek
and powerful, and gleamingly expensive, its paintwork
was a shining light grey, almost silver, reminding her disturbingly of the eyes of the man in the managing director's office—eyes that had looked at her with such
contempt at first. But then that expression had swiftly
changed to something much more worrying.

The car was in the MD's private space too, she now
realised, struggling with the shake in her hand that made
it difficult to insert her key in the ignition. It was parked
in the spot that had previously been reserved solely for
the use of Owen's late father—a space which must now,
by rights, belong to Owen himself. Which, logic told her,
bringing with it a wave of nausea, meant that there was
only one person it could belong to—and that made
matters all the worse.

Perhaps if she had been more aware of her surroundings on her arrival, if she'd been thinking
straighter, she would have noticed it then, and its el-
egantly alien presence might have made her pause to re-
consider her plan of action. But the truth was that she
had been blind to everything but that plan. In fact, she
had actively encouraged her anger on the journey here,
feeding the flames, so that she hadn't even noticed that
Owen's car wasn't even in the car park at all.

She hadn't even paused to look around her, Saffron reflected, sighing with relief as the slightly untrustworthy engine caught, and she let the brake out with nervous haste, not even glancing behind to see if her pursuer had come out of the building. She only wanted to get out of here without any further confrontation with the owner of that sleek, powerful vehicle, she told herself. Her stomach twisted into tight, painful knots of apprehension as every sense became tensely alert, ears straining for the shout she expected as she headed for the exit; unwillingly she contrasted her speedy departure, like a dog with its tail between its legs, with her confident, even cocky arrival such a short time earlier.

Then, fired up with determination and anger, she had barely allowed herself time to park the car before she was out of it and striding towards the main entrance, her brisk, forceful movements mirroring the state of her thoughts.

'Hey!'

The shout cut into her thoughts, sounding clearly even above the noise of the engine, and the car swerved dangerously as her hands clenched on the wheel. A swift, nervous glance in the rearview mirror confirmed her instinctive fear, her stomach twisting painfully as she saw the way that letting her mind wander had slowed her responses, stilling her foot on the accelerator. Alerted by the sound of the engine, her pursuer had come out of the building and was heading purposefully across the car park towards her.

'Wait! I want to——'

The rest of his words were drowned in the roar of the car as, heedless of safety or concern for her elderly vehicle, she rammed her right foot down to the floor. She knew very well what he wanted—he had made that only too plain—and she had no intention of waiting around to endure any more of his blatantly lecherous remarks.

It was just as she swung out of the car park and on to the main road that she glanced back one last time and saw the way he had halted, bending to pick up something from the ground.

Kate's shoes, she reflected ruefully, wondering if, as in the Cinderella story, he thought he might use them as evidence to track her down. The problem was, though, that *he* was no sort of Prince Charming—quite the opposite—and if he did turn out to be who she suspected then she would need more than just a fairy godmother to get her out of a *very* sticky situation.

CHAPTER TWO

'FOR God's sake, Saffron—how many times do I have to apologise?'

Owen pushed impatient hands through his hair—hair that was not quite as dark as that of the man in the MD's office, Saffron noted inconsequentially. His had been black as a raven's wing where Owen's was just a deep brown. That should have warned her, but she'd been too angry to think straight, and after all she had been expecting Owen to be there—hadn't anticipated the possibility of anyone else being in the office.

'Saffy, are you listening? I said I'm sorry.'

He didn't *sound* penitent, Saffron reflected privately. If anything, he was quite the opposite—almost aggressive, in fact.

'We had a date, Owen. I bought a new dress——'

The words dried in her throat as the thought of just what else she'd bought slid into her mind, bringing with it an all too vivid picture of the scarlet wisps of silk that she had pushed firmly to the bottom of the washing-basket. She doubted that she could ever wear them again when just the thought of putting them on awoke uncomfortable memories of the scene in the office, the sensual amusement in that appalling man's voice. In fact, she didn't know what had possessed her to buy them in the first place. They were a million miles away from the sort of thing she normally chose.

'I waited for hours.'

'I *know*.' Owen sounded positively snappish now. 'But I promised you dinner at Le Figaro and——' an airy wave of his hand indicated their elegant surroundings '—I'm keeping my promise.'

'Twenty-four hours late!'

Saffron couldn't bite back the retort. Owen was the one who had stood her up, and yet he was behaving as if *she* was the offender. If he'd kept the date as arranged, she would never have gone to his office in a temper and made such a spectacle of herself.

'Saff, you know how important this takeover is to me! I couldn't keep our date yesterday because the big man turned up without warning.'

'The big man?'

Saffron fought hard to keep her voice under control, but the rising tide of colour in her cheeks was a different matter. Try as she might, she couldn't avoid the logical connection that her mind was making between Owen's words and the hateful character she had encountered in the MD's office. She had suspected this, had known that there wasn't really a hope that she could be wrong, but to hear it confirmed by Owen was almost more than she could cope with right now.

'Niall Forrester himself. Oh, come on, Saff! Where have you been for the past month? Niall Forrester owns Forrester Leisure, and Forrester Leisure——'

'Is considering buying Richards' Rockets—I know *that*.'

She knew only too well that Owen, whose interests lay in a very different direction, had been delighted when the huge international corporation had shown an interest in the small, rather rundown family business that he had inherited from his father six months before.

'After all, you've talked about nothing else all month.'

She found it impossible to erase the tartness from her voice, but, well-launched on his major preoccupation, Owen seemed oblivious to the sharpness of her tone.

'So, you'll understand that when Niall Forrester himself rang to say he was coming up to Kirkham to look at the factory I just had to be there to meet him—and take him out to dinner in the evening. He kept me busy, I can tell you. He wanted to know everything there was to know—I didn't have time to think——'

Or to ring and explain, Saffron reflected with a touch of asperity. But at the forefront of her mind was a more pressing worry.

'And this Niall Forrester—the "big man"——'

The description fitted. Even sitting down, he had looked decidedly impressive, and the width of the straight, powerful shoulders under the immaculately fitted navy suit had been evidence of a formidable physique that, if she had had her wits about her, she should have known could not possibly have belonged to Owen.

'Where is he now?'

'Back in London, I expect. He said he'd seen all he wanted to see at the factory.'

Hastily Saffron tried to convert the choking sensation that had assailed her into an innocuous cough. Niall Forrester had seen everything he wanted and more! But at least it seemed that she could relax about one thing. Obviously, whatever his feelings about her appearance in the MD's office, Forrester had said nothing about it to Owen. Of course, he wouldn't know her name, but he could have asked the receptionist. If he'd described her, Beth would have known who he meant. The colour flooding her cheeks deepened hotly at the thought of just how he might have described her.

'You're not exactly chatty, Saff!' Owen sounded decidedly peeved. 'Is this because you haven't forgiven me for last night? You're not going to sulk all evening, are you?'

'I'm not sulking!'

Saffron was indignant. Clearly Owen thought that he had apologised, but to her mind it seemed that what he'd really done was bring home to her the way that she came in second place in his life, after his business interests. From being angry about the way he had stood her up, she was now forced to wonder whether in fact his non-appearance last night had been a lucky escape in some ways. After the decision about their relationship that she had come to, only so recently, it was disturbing, to say the least, to find that her attitude towards him had shifted ground.

In fact, ever since Owen had appeared at her flat, she had been seeing him in a very different light. It was more than just annoyance at the way he had stood her up, though obviously that had a lot to do with it. Suddenly almost everything he said seemed to irritate her.

'I've—just got something on my mind. I'd planned on working on the accounts this evening. Things are really getting a bit tight, and——'

'Oh, they'll keep until tomorrow. After all, a tiny business like yours can't have many real problems— nothing compared to the white elephant of a factory my father left me lumbered with. I mean—who wants to buy fireworks nowadays?'

Once more he was launched on his own concerns. Listening to him, Saffron had to bite down hard on her lower lip in order to keep back an angry response. Owen had always had a tendency to be like this, but somehow tonight it seemed much more infuriating than usual. Was she just feeling unsettled after the disturbing meeting at the factory that morning, or did it go deeper than that?

At that moment her thought processes stopped dead, because in the second that she had looked away, needing to distract herself from Owen's soliloquy and the urge to tell him to shut up, her attention had been drawn to a flurry of activity at the entrance to the restaurant and then, unbelievingly, inexorably, to the tall figure of the man who had just come in.

She recognised him immediately. There was no mistaking that jet-black gleaming hair, the straight, firm shoulders, the arrogant, upright carriage that had impressed her even when he was sitting down. Seen on his feet like this, that dark, sleek head towering inches above the head waiter—who, recognising intuitively the innate self-assurance and air of power that only a great deal of money could buy, was buzzing around him like a bee around an open honey-pot—he was even more imposing, a forceful, vital figure of a man who would always be noticed the moment he walked into a room. Even through the haze of shock that clouded her brain she was well aware of the fact that hers weren't the only pair of female eyes that had noted his arrival—noted it and lingered in frank appreciation.

'Forrester!'

Dimly, with a sense of terrible inevitability, she heard Owen's exclamation confirm her earlier fears, depriving her of any possible weakly lingering hope that she might have been mistaken about the identity of the man in the managing director's office.

'But I thought he'd gone back to London.' Her voice was an uncomfortable croak as she struggled to believe that this was actually happening, that he could be here—now. If he saw them—saw her——

'So did I. Something must have kept him. Hey, Forrester! Niall!'

To Saffron's horror, Owen was out of his seat, waving a hand to attract the other man's attention.

'I'll ask him to join us—you should meet him. Forrester—over here!'

'Owen!' Saffron whispered through clenched teeth,
but it was too late. Owen's actions had drawn Niall
Forrester's gaze, those unforgettable light grey eyes narrowing slightly as they focused on his face from across
the room.

He was not at all pleased at being accosted in this way,
Saffron realised, seeing with a twist of apprehension the
way that his dark brows drew together sharply, indi-
cating an annoyed response that had her shrinking down
in her chair, fearful of that cold-eyed scrutiny being
turned on her too. Perhaps he would ignore Owen, take
a table at the far side of the room.

'Over here!' Owen tried again, beckoning osten-
tatiously, in the same moment that Saffron realised just
how ridiculous she was being, hiding away like this, as
if she was some small, hunted animal.

With an angry reproof to herself, she straightened up
again, and then immediately wished she hadn't as the
slight movement caught Niall Forrester's attention, and
with a sinking heart she saw his expression change
swiftly. Even from this distance she could see the fierce,
almost predatory gleam of triumph that lit up those pale
eyes, turning them to silver and making all the nerves
in the pit of her stomach twist into tight, painful knots
of panic. It was all that she could do to remain in her
seat, only suppressing the urge to push back her chair
and run with a supreme effort.

But he was coming towards them now, his stride as
determined and purposeful as his expression, and with
a bitter sense of despair she knew that there was no way
she could avoid the confrontation that was approaching
as swiftly and inexorably as the darkness that was gathering outside. If she *did* run, she had no doubt that he
would come after her, would catch up with her without
any difficulty. And that that would result in a scene even

worse than the one she now anticipated with such dread, she acknowledged miserably, wiping suddenly damp palms nervously on her napkin, convinced that the diners at the next table must hear how heavily her heart was pounding.

'Richards. Good evening——'

The sound of that smooth, attractive voice was like a blow to Saffron's head, the single phrase reverberating over and over in her disturbed thoughts. She had only heard perhaps ninety-five or a hundred words in those deep, slightly husky tones, and yet she felt as if every note of it, every shaded inflexion was etched into her brain in red-hot strokes.

'Would you like to join us?' Owen was totally oblivious to Saffron's discomfiture. 'It's no fun dining alone.'

'Thank you—I'd appreciate that.'

The smoothness of Niall Forrester's tone made Saffron blink hard in shock. Had she been seeing things a moment earlier? Or had her own nervousness made her misinterpret his expression? Certainly, there was no sign of the cold-eyed look she had seen on his face; now he was all affable approachability, oozing social ease from every pore.

'I'd anticipated a solitary meal, so some company would be welcome.'

The words were directed at Owen, but Saffron had caught the swift flicker of a glance in her direction, a look that left her in no doubt that he was only too well aware of her presence.

He *was* even more impressive standing up. She had tried to convince herself that the image she had created of him in her mind had been exaggerated, blown up out of all proportion by her own feelings about their meeting, but now she had to admit that, if anything, she had erred on the side of moderation. He had changed his clothes, but the dark suit he now wore was every bit as sleek and expensive as the first one, its superbly tailored lines clinging to a lean but strongly muscled frame, and under the fine material his waist and hips had the slimness of an athlete, showing that he kept himsef very fit. Standing beside Owen like this, he made the other man, who was a good six feet in his socks, look slight and underweight. And those eyes! Saffron kept her own gaze firmly fixed on her plate for fear of meeting the silver intensity of Niall Forrester's scrutiny.

'Won't you introduce me to your charming companion?'

Hastily Saffron tried to impose some control over her expression as Owen, belatedly recalling her presence at the table, turned in her direction.

'Of course—this is Saffron Ruane. Saffy, this is Niall Forrester. I told you about his interest in Dad's factory.'

'I remember.'

She managed a small, tight smile, feeling as if her face might actually crack if she tried any more, and, because courtesy demanded it, she held out her hand in greeting. It was taken in a warm, firm grasp that folded around her fingers, enclosing them in a way that in any other person would have inspired confidence and trust. To her consternation, this time it had exactly the opposite effect. She felt as if a live electric wire had coiled around her fingers, sending burning shockwaves pulsing across her palm and along every nerve in her arm so that it was all she could do not to snatch her hand away again with a cry of distress.

And in the moment that his broad, strong hand closed over hers she found herself looking into those clear, steel-grey eyes, her gaze held transfixed, held with such magnetic force that for a second or two she felt physically

dizzy and actually swayed slightly in her seat, knowing
that if she had been standing her legs would have given
way beneath her and she would have fallen to the floor.

'Miss Ruane——' A slight inclination of his dark head
acknowledged her, nothing about his expression or de-
meanour giving any indication that he recognised her.
'I hope you don't think that I'm intruding?'

The act of polite concern, nothing more, was near-
perfect, almost too much so, and if she hadn't been so
excruciatingly aware of the circumstances of their previous meeting, Saffron knew that she wouldn't have been
able to fault it.

'Not at all——' What else could she say? 'Won't you
sit down?'

Saffron took the opportunity to remove her hand from
his with a rush of relief, turning the movement into a
gesture towards the empty chair opposite in order to
cover the rather abrupt way in which she snatched her
fingers away, unable to bear his touch any longer.

Or was she worrying unnecessarily? she couldn't help
but wonder, as Niall seated himself. After all, he had
only seen her for a very few minutes in the office—and
she very much doubted that, for the most of them, his
attention had been concentrated on her *face*! The
memory of just what *had* held his interest had her
reaching for her glass and taking a hasty gulp of her
wine, hoping that its cool sharpness would halt the rush
of colour to her cheeks, and she was grateful for the
appearance of the waiter at Niall's side, providing a
welcome distraction from her betraying response.

She might have known that Niall Forrester would attract such prompt and almost obsequious service, she
reflected wryly, seeing the waiter's overly polite concern.
He was the sort of man who emanated an aura of power
and control—and he looked as if he would tip gener-

ously, she added with a touch of cynicism, recalling just how long she and Owen had had to wait before anyone came to take *their* order.

'I'll pass on the starter, then we'll all be at the same stage.' Clearly, Niall had noted their almost empty plates. 'And bring another bottle of wine.'

'Oh, but——'

Saffron had been about to protest that Owen was driving, and that she had no head for anything other than a couple of glasses, but even as she spoke Niall forestalled her, lifting their original bottle of wine from its ice-bucket and refilling their half-empty glasses.

'Thank you,' she was obliged to murmur, struggling against an impulse to lift her glass and fling its expensive contents in his face.

'Not at all,' he responded smoothly. 'In fact, I'd like you to consider yourselves my guests tonight—my thanks for a most interesting day at the factory.'

Was she being unduly sensitive? Saffron couldn't help wondering. Or *had* there been a worrying emphasis on that 'interesting', turning it into something that made her shift uncomfortably in her seat?

'It was my pleasure.'

Owen tried to match the other man's easy assurance but only managed to sound oily and insincere, and the way he had to lean forward as he spoke in order to make his presence felt made Saffron aware of the way that, while his remarks had *seemed* to have been aimed at them both, Niall had concentrated that silvery gaze on her face alone, making her feel like the selected victim, deliberately singled out by a ruthless predator.

'I must admit that I'm surprised to see you here tonight.' She forced the words out, determined not to let him see how much he worried her. 'I thought you'd be over halfway back to London by now.'

'That was my original intention, but I changed my mind and decided to stay overnight—do some sightseeing.'

'Sightseeing? In Kirkham?' Saffron didn't bother to hide her scepticism.

'Oh, you'd be surprised,' Niall returned, with a smile that made every nerve in her body tense uneasily. It wasn't humour that lit those pale eyes from within, but a hint of taunting triumph, that made her think worryingly of a hunting cat sitting patiently outside a mouse-hole, waiting for the unwary rodent to venture out. 'For a sleepy little Northern town, this place has some unexpected attractions...'

That silvery gaze slid deliberately to her face, and Saffron's breath caught in her throat as she saw that the mocking glint had brightened but not warmed those light eyes, so that they glittered with the brilliance of ice in the sun.

'Wouldn't you agree, Miss Ruane?'

As he spoke he looked straight into her eyes, that smile making a mockery of her earlier foolish hope that perhaps he hadn't recognised her. He was playing with her, well aware of her discomfort; he was enjoying watching her squirm.

'Oh, Saffy isn't a local girl,' Owen put in cheerfully. 'She only came to live in Kirkham a couple of years ago.'

'That's a pity.' The cool grey eyes never left Saffron's troubled brown ones. 'I had rather hoped that you might be able to show me around.'

His tone was dangerously soft, worryingly gentle, making Saffron think uncomfortably of the cat she had compared him to earlier—the soft fur of its paws concealing the powerful, tearing claws.

'I was sure that you were the sort of girl who knows the best places to go for a special night out.'

A special night out. This time there was no mistaking the subtle deepening of his drawling tones on those words, forcing her to recall how she had used them herself only a few hours before. And the implication behind what he had said was painfully clear too, to anyone who had seen the insultingly knowing smile on his face when he had spoken of customers and terms. She could have little doubt as to what sort of nights out were in his disgusting mind.

'On the contrary,' she returned sharply. 'I'm very much a stay-at-home, Mr Forrester. Not at all a clubs-and-pubs sort of woman.'

'That wasn't exactly what I had in mind,' he disconcerted her by saying.

'Well, if it's night-life you want——' Owen put in, anxious, Saffron knew, to give a plug to the night-club he hoped to buy a half-share in.

'Not really.' Niall barely spared him a glance. 'Look, Richards, is that a friend of yours?' A nod of his dark head indicated a table on the other side of the room, where a man Saffron vaguely recognised was waving to gain Owen's attention. 'Hadn't you better see what he wants?'

He didn't even watch Owen leave, instead concentrating all his attention on Saffron, continuing the conversation as if the interruption had never happened.

'I can assure you that I wouldn't think of hiding you away in some smoky, dimly lit club. A beauty such as yours should be seen in the full light of day.'

Saffron's soft mouth parted on a gasp of astonishment, both at the arrogance of his dismissal of Owen and at the outrageous compliment.

'Are you trying to flirt with me, Mr Forrester?'

His smile was a challenge, the intent gaze of those steely eyes seeming to draw her to him like some irresistible magnet, holding her transfixed, unable to look away.

'On the contrary—flirting is a frivolous occupation, meant only light-heartedly. I am deadly serious——'

That voice would charm the birds out of the trees, Saffron thought hazily. Low and huskily sensual, it was pitched so as to make her feel as if she was the only woman in the room—in the world—and his words were for her alone. And it was working!

In spite of her determination to resist, fired by the knowledge of the low opinion he really had of her, it seemed as if her surroundings, the buzz of conversation from the other diners, had all faded from her awareness, blending into a multi-coloured blur, so that all she was aware of was a pair of hypnotic grey eyes and a silkily seductive voice.

'You must know that you are an exceptionally lovely woman—such dark hair and eyes, and a face like a Madonna.'

'Oh, really!' With an effort Saffron struggled to break free of the hypnotic hold he had on her. 'Now you're exaggerating!'

She felt desperately out of her depth. It was as if she had been floating lazily on a sunlit sea and had suddenly realised that the shore was much further away than she had thought, with the current growing ominously rougher. The concentration of his gaze, the intensity of that huskily seductive voice, were more suited to the intimacy of a bedroom than this public place. As her mind made the connection between the man before her and the thought of the sensual surroundings of a bedroom her thoughts reeled, the image working on them like some powerfully intoxicating cocktail.

'I never exaggerate.'

Niall Forrester dismissed her protest with the same casual indifference he might have used to flick away a fly that had come too near his face, and the gleam that lit deep in his eyes told her that he was well aware of her struggle to break away from the hold he seemed to have on her. That hold was as delicate as a spider's web and yet as powerful as if she were actually confined by steel cables. The rational part of her mind was screaming at her that all she had to do was look away, look at someone else, but she found it impossible to move.

'And in your case I have no need to. Though I have to admit...'

A tiny flicker of his eyes, downwards over the simple navy dress she wore, and a slight deepening of that smile, curling his mouth up at the corners, acted as a danger signal, warning Saffron that she wouldn't like what was to come.

'That that particular shade of blue you're wearing is not perhaps the most flattering to someone of your dramatic colouring. I would have thought that something warmer—perhaps red...'

He caught the flare of apprehension in her eyes and the smile grew, becoming tauntingly triumphant as Saffron's start of shock betrayed her awareness of the direction in which he was heading.

'Scarlet, possibly.' He drew the first word out so that it was a softly sensual sound on his tongue, almost a caress in itself. 'Yes, I can see you in scarlet—something in silk——'

'Oh, *please*!' Saffron put in hastily, loading her tone with sarcasm. She'd had enough of this cat-and-mouse act; it was time to fight back. 'You have to be joking! I only ever wore scarlet silk once—never again!'

She gave a carefully delicate shudder of distaste, dark brown eyes meeting silver, hers burning with defiance, her chin lifting challengingly.

'It was a dreadful mistake—one I have no intention of repeating—*ever.*'

The deliberate emphasis on the final word was like a verbal throwing down of a gauntlet in front of Niall, an attempt to throw him off-balance, but to Saffron's annoyance he didn't react in the way she had anticipated. If anything, her challenge seemed to have amused rather than disconcerted him, and that smile grew in a way that she found positively hateful.

'I can't believe that. I can picture you in scarlet——'

The gleam in those pale eyes told her just *how* he was picturing her, and it took all Saffron's self-control not to react to the almost lascivious pleasure that was so clearly stamped on the hard-boned features before her. Her fingers itched to lash out and wipe it from his face and she had to clamp them together tightly in her lap in order not to give in to the impulse.

'And, in my opinion, it wouldn't be any sort of a mistake at all.'

'Really?' Using every ounce of acting ability she possessed, Saffron injected the word with an icy hauteur. 'Well, I'm afraid that you're never likely to see me in any such thing.'

After this, she wouldn't be able to bear to wear the scarlet silk underwear ever again. She would sooner die! Even just to see it would remind her unbearably of the look in his eyes, that hateful smile, his voice...

'So, we'll just have to agree to differ on this.'

She knew that by defying him like this she was risking his anger, possibly even the fact that he might call her bluff and tell Owen everything, but she couldn't stop herself. She had to stand up to him, give as good as she got.

For a carefully timed moment he kept her hanging, waiting for his response, then, just at the point where she thought that she would scream if he didn't say something, he lifted his broad shoulders in a nonchalant shrug.

'So we will,' he said easily, adding in a tone so soft that only she could hear, 'For now.'

At that moment the waiter appeared with their meal, Owen returning to the table at the same time, and Saffron welcomed the interruption thankfully as a chance to gather her thoughts and try to cling on to the shattered remains of her composure. She knew exactly what Niall Forrester was up to. He had made it only too plain that he appreciated—and enjoyed—the possibilities of some rather nasty emotional blackmail, was well aware of how uncomfortable she would be at the prospect of Owen finding out about the fact that they had already met— and in what circumstances!

The problem was that he couldn't be more wrong. In the same second that she had considered the possibility of Niall telling Owen everything, she had realised just how little it worried her. All through the evening—in fact, ever since Owen had stood her up—she had had second, and third—even fourth thoughts about their relationship, and now she knew that there no longer was a relationship to worry about. She didn't care if Owen found out—and yet she still felt threatened. And that was what really worried her.

Earlier she had thought of Niall Forrester as a cat sitting outside a mousehole, and now she could be in no doubt as to just who was his prey. This particular sleek, dark-coated feline clearly had all the patience in the world when it came to hunting, and he wanted her to know that he was prepared to play a waiting game, showing no sign of pouncing until she put herself in a position of weakness by venturing too far outside the safety of her hiding place.

The problem was that she didn't know quite what she was hiding from. It wasn't any threat of exposure to Owen, however embarrassing that might be, instead it was something much more specific to Niall himself. Simply by existing, by awakening this unwilling, unwelcome response in her, he seemed to threaten her security, her peace of mind. It was as if she were one of the fireworks produced in Owen's factory, and someone had placed a lighted match to her own personal fuse. That fuse was burning worryingly swiftly, and she had the frightening feeling that in a very short space of time something was going to blow up right in her face.

CHAPTER THREE

'SAFFRON is an unusual name—though I suspect that you're more than tired of people commenting on it.'

'Oh, well, it was my aunt who suggested it. It came from a favourite song of hers.' Saffron was determined not to let him see how exactly he had hit upon the truth. 'And by the time they'd named five other daughters my parents had run out of names that they liked.'

To his credit, Niall didn't even blink, which was surprising. Many people were so accustomed to the idea of small families that the thought of six children—and all of the same sex—had them reeling back in astonishment. Owen had almost had to pick himself up off the floor when she had told him.

'Saffy's the youngest of this ridiculously huge family.' Owen had grown tired of being kept out of the conversation. 'Seven women! It's no wonder her father buried himself in his books.' Reaching for the wine-bottle, he refilled his glass.

'Don't you think you'd better go easy?' Saffron put in hastily, and was subjected to a look of such withering scorn that the protest died on her lips.

'Lighten up, Saff! No one likes a killjoy.'

Owen's retort was accompanied by a swift, expressive glance in Niall Forrester's direction. It was a look of pure conspiracy, man to man, of banding together in the face of female constraint in a way that made her prickle with irritation.

'But you're driving me home.'

'I'll be fine——'

And her concern was dismissed, so that unless she persisted, creating a nasty little scene in front of the interestedly watchful Niall, she had no option but to remain uncomfortably silent.

Perhaps in the past she might have shrugged off Owen's behaviour, possibly even telling herself that she might have over-reacted. But tonight she found that his rudeness had her boiling inside, anger searing through her like a red-hot tide so that she had to bite her lip hard in order not to tell him exactly what she thought of him. In fact, looking at his smiling self-absorbed face as he returned once more to his favourite subject of the proposed takeover, she was forced to wonder what she had ever seen in him.

Could she really have ever considered sleeping with this man? But hadn't that been exactly what she had planned on doing—last night, at least? Barely twenty-four hours ago, she realised, surreptitiously consulting the slim gold watch on her wrist, she had been so sure about everything. Now, she no longer knew what she felt. It all seemed to have happened since Niall Forrester had come into her life.

'I'm sorry——' Niall's sharp eyes had caught the tiny movement as she checked the time. 'We're boring you.'

'Not at all.' She hoped that her cool tones would communicate that nothing he could do would trouble her in the least. 'I appreciate that you have plenty to talk to Owen about. After all, it's his company that you're going to buy.'

'Possibly.' The single word held a suggestion of doubt, a reminder that all was not yet certain. 'If I decide I want it...'

Because she was already on edge, that, 'If...I want it' seemed to catch of Saffron's raw nerves.

'Is that really what life's about—getting what you want?'

'Isn't it?' He questioned coolly. 'I think if you asked the majority of people they'd say that most of their days are spent dreaming of something they want—trying to obtain it. I'm not unusual in that—only in that perhaps I know more clearly than most what I do want, and that when I see what I want, I go for it. I make sure nothing stands in the way of my getting it.'

The way he looked straight into her eyes as he spoke, a curl at the corner of his mouth, made Saffron think uncomfortably of his words that morning. 'You're exactly what I've been looking for——'

'And what if, when you've got your hands on whatever it is, it turns out not to be so desirable after all?'

His smile mocked her indignation, almost as if he knew the thoughts that were in her mind. 'Oh, then I'd just turn and walk away.'

'No backward glances?'

'Looking back is just a waste of time. If you want to make any progress, the only way is forward.'

She wished he would look away from her, turn the silvery force of those pale eyes on someone else. They might have started out talking about Owen's company and, ostensibly, to anyone not in the know, it might appear that they were still discussing just that, but Saffron was hypersensitive to the dangerous undercurrents in the atmosphere around her, uncomfortably aware of the other possible interpretation of Niall's words.

'And does that apply to emotional matters as well as business deals?'

She felt she didn't need to ask the question, already anticipating what the answer would be.

'So far I've never encountered anything that I couldn't resist or leave behind with no regrets.'

'Anything or anyone?'

Niall's only response was a slight inclination of his dark head, but a worrying gleam in those silvery eyes made her decide that it would be much safer to move the talk back on to the original topic.

'And do you think you'll want Richards' Rockets?'

As she had hoped, the question brought Owen back into the conversation and she was able to withdraw, sit back and watch as once more the two men became absorbed in their discussion.

The problem was that she didn't experience the relief she had hoped for. Only moments before she had wanted Niall Forrester to turn his attention elsewhere and leave her in peace, but now that he had, perversely, she felt irritated by the ease with which he seemed able to dismiss her from his thoughts. The chocolate torte which the waiter had brought her, together with another bottle of wine, now seemed much too rich for her taste, and she laid her spoon down, painfully aware of the fact that there was really nothing wrong with the sweet, only with her mood.

She couldn't stop her gaze from lingering on the man opposite, on the sculpted planes of his face, shadowed softly in the flickering candlelight, on the jet darkness of his hair, the unexpected softness of his mouth. Her eyes followed every gesture of his hands as he ate, talked, poured the wine. Those pale grey eyes of his were turned away from her now, but in her mind she could see them in all the changeable moods that, even after such a short acquaintance, she could recognise—the cold, steely glitter that could turn so swiftly to the warm glow of polished silver, or darken with something she couldn't—or didn't dare—put a name to.

'Is there something wrong with your food?'

'What?'

Niall's voice had been soft and low, but even so the sound of it jolted Saffron from the sensual trance that had held her. It was as if the gentle warmth of the candle-flames had spread throughout the room, growing in intensity, heating the blood in her veins so that she felt as if she was adrift on a golden, glowing tide, the sight and sounds of the other diners fading to a blur on the edges of her consciousness, every nerve, every sense centring on Niall Forrester, like a compass needle drawn irresistibly to the North.

'I'll send it back if it's not right——'

'Oh, no—no, it's fine.'

I'll send it back, she noted resentfully. Niall Forrester had well and truly taken over the evening.

'It's just—that I haven't as much appetite as I thought.'

For food only, a rogue part of her mind commented. Other appetites were not so easily appeased. In fact, with those silvery eyes on her once more, the way he was leaning towards her bringing him so close that she caught the scent of some musky cologne he wore, she felt as if every inch of her skin was newly sensitised, and a previously unknown sensation was uncoiling in the pit of her stomach, as if some sensuous snake-like creature had been sleeping heavily but was now starting to awake...

'Eyes too big for my stomach!' she managed on a shaky laugh.

'Then perhaps we should think about leaving.'

Was she being unduly sensitive? Saffron wondered. Or was it just his physical position, the concentration of his attention on her, that seemed to make that 'we' exclude Owen, who, having tackled a large portion of his favourite Black Forest gateau, was now draining the last of his wine?

'Yes,' he said on a sigh of satisfaction. 'Better be going. Waiter!'

'Let me——' Once more Niall took charge, catching the waiter's eye with an ease that made the other man's waving hand look gauche and unsophisticated. In fact, it was rather over the top, even for Owen, Saffron reflected, her attention caught suddenly.

'Most gracious of you——'

It was the first couple of words, with the hint of slurring, that alerted her, making her turn a concerned frown on him, to see his flushed face and overbright eyes. Her fears were confirmed as Owen got to his feet unsteadily, swaying and clutching at the table for support.

'Owen—you're drunk!'

'Not at all!' He gave a foolish grin. 'Just a bit mellow.'

'But you're not fit to drive!' She thought despairingly of the long journey home, the lack of buses, the prohibitive cost of a taxi.

'Perhaps I could help?'

Did this man have ears like a bat? Her conversation with Owen had been conducted in a furious whisper, while he was occupied with the waiter and his credit card, but he was still very much aware of what was happening.

'I have my car here—I could take you both home.'

'But—didn't you——?'

Anticipating her question, Niall shook his dark head. 'I'm well under the limit—you'll be perfectly safe.'

And, looking into those clear grey eyes Saffron knew that he spoke the absolute truth. He had been decidedly abstemious, she recalled. If only Owen had been equally restrained!

'I can drive!' Owen protested.

'I don't think so!' Niall's voice was warm with humour, and he moved swiftly to support the other man as he lurched clumsily away from the table. 'Come on, mate—this way——'

Owen was more intoxicated than Saffron had first realised, and in the first flurry of activity involved in getting him out of the restaurant, across the courtyard and into Niall's car—the same sleek, grey vehicle that she had seen in the factory car park—she had little time to think of anything beyond a strong sense of gratitude for Niall's calm, helpful presence.

She doubted that she would have been able to cope without him, without his physical strength to support Owen's unsteady progress, the amused but firm tact with which he distracted the other man from his determination to drive home, and the final intuitive sensitivity he showed in personally supervising Owen's delivery into the care of his disapproving mother, enabling Saffron to remain in the car and out of sight. She was well aware of just what Mrs Richards would think if she knew of her presence.

'At last!' Niall exclaimed, sliding back into the driving-seat and pushing both hands through his hair with a sigh of relief. 'I thought we'd never get rid of him.'

'Thanks for seeing him to the door for me. If Ma Richards had realised I was with him she'd have blamed me for the state he's in.'

'She wouldn't believe him capable of getting that way by himself?' Niall slanted a quizzical glance in her direction as he turned the key in the ignition, bringing the powerful engine to swift, purring life.

'Her precious Owen?' Saffron assumed an expression of exaggerated horror. 'Not on your life! He can do no wrong—except for the fact that he's seeing me. Mrs Richards has never really liked me—she doesn't think I'm quite good enough for her only child. As a matter of fact,' she added, impelled by scrupulous honesty, 'he's never really been quite so silly before.'

'No?' Niall sounded unconvinced and dismissively uninterested. 'Where to now? Where do you live—Saffron?'

But Saffron's sudden silence was not because she hadn't heard his question. Instead she had been struck by something in his tone, something distinctly cagey and with a dark note that made her nerves twist in sudden apprehension. As the sleek car pulled away from the kerb she heard again in her thoughts that expressive, 'At last!' and found herself looking back at the evening with fresh eyes, seeing belatedly how Niall had kept Owen's attention, picturing him chatting easily, summoning the waiter, ordering wine—refilling the other man's glass...

Suddenly she was sitting upright in her seat, her body taut with indignation, rejection, and something very close to fear.

'It was you!'

Niall didn't try to deny the accusation. He didn't even bother to ask exactly what she meant, but simply turned and gave her a swift, unrevealing smile before apparently concentrating his attention on the road ahead.

'It was you! *You* got Owen drunk quite deliberately! You poured him all that wine——'

'No one forced him to drink it,' Niall put in, his carefully reasonable tone only incensing her further. 'I didn't exactly pour the damn stuff down his throat.'

'You might just as well have done! Owen doesn't get presented with that sort of vintage every day of his life—certainly not in such quantities! And you know perfectly well that he wouldn't have wanted to offend you by refusing.'

'I'd have thought better of him if he had,' Niall commented drily, but Saffron wasn't listening. Her mind had gone into overdrive, whirling frantically as she tried to see just what this meant to her—because she was sud-

denly uncomfortably certain that Niall Forrester hadn't
got Owen drunk just for his own twisted amusement.

'You knew that I was concerned! I said that I needed
Owen to drive me home, and yet you continued to ply
him with wine——'

But he had accepted her own refusal to drink any more
with perfect equanimity.

'Why——?' she began, her strangled tone revealing
that she already suspected what his answer was going to
be, and didn't like it at all. 'Why?'

Niall turned another of those mocking, knowing smiles
on her, his face half-shadowed and eerie in the light of
the streetlamps.

'Oh, come on, Saffron,' he reproved gently. 'You don't
need to ask that. You know exactly what I had planned.
I had to get Owen out of the way because I wanted to
be alone with you. But of course you knew that, because, after all, it was just what you wanted too.'

'I wanted——' Saffron choked on the words in her
haste to get out an indignant refusal. 'I wanted no such
thing!'

'Oh, but you did, sweetheart. I'm not blind. I could
see it—read it in your face. It was there in the way you
couldn't take your eyes off me, the way you tried to play
it oh, so cool and failed miserably—the way you snapped
when I spoke to you but sulked when I turned my attention away.'

'You arrogant pig!'

The knowledge that she was using her anger as a de-
fence against his accusations made her tone even more
aggressive than she had intended. The problem was that
she couldn't deny the facts—but it was the interpretation
he had put on them that was so infuriating.

Or was it? When her own mind played traitor, flinging
at her a series of sensual images, reminding her of the

effect Niall had had on her, that sensation of something awakening deep inside, she was forced to doubt her own conviction. Was that what he had seen in her face? She was grateful for the shadows that hid the rush of hot colour into her face at the thought.

'It wasn't like that,' she muttered, shifting uncomfortably in her seat.

'No? Seemed that way to me. Enough to make me want to test out the theory, anyway. And as young Mr Richards was something of an obstacle to that I—provided him with an excuse to leave us alone at the earliest possible opportunity. I think he enjoyed the experience, and there won't be too much embarrassment on his part.'

'On his part!' Saffron exploded. 'Owen wasn't the only one who was manipulated! How the hell do you think *I* feel? What about *my* embarrassment? Or don't my feelings count for anything in all this?'

For a long, intent second Niall took his eyes off the road and subjected her furious face to a sharply assessing scrutiny that made her skin crawl in response.

'On the contrary, it was your feelings I was considering.'

'My feelings! You decide that you know what I want, without so much as consulting me, deliberately get my boyfriend drunk so that I end up alone with you, whether I like it or not, and then you have the nerve to say you were *considering my feelings*! Consideration doesn't come into it! Pure, arrogant selfishness is more like it!'

'Oh, come on, honey!' Niall wasn't in the least bit rattled by her outburst. 'You know I made things easier for you. It would have been *embarrassing*, to say the least——' with silky deliberation he emphasised the word she had flung at him so angrily '—to have had to say to your boyfriend, "Look, I know I came with you, but I'm leaving with someone else." Don't you think?'

As Saffron's mouth actually gaped in shock, the knowledge of the fact that she no longer wanted to continue seeing Owen depriving her of the ability to form any angry retort, he continued smoothly, 'Especially if he'd paid for your dinner—so I took care of that too.'

'And you think that for the price of one meal you've *bought* me! That isn't so much Old Man as positively barbaric! What are you? Some sort of primitive Neanderthal?'

'At the moment, what I am is hopelessly lost,' Niall stunned her by replying. 'How about getting down off your high-horse and giving me directions?'

'Directions?' Thoroughly confused by the change of subject, and bewildered by the teasing note that had suddenly appeared in his voice, Saffron could only stare blankly. 'To where?'

'To your home, of course.' The patient resignation that shaded his tone riled her further. 'I did say I would drive you back, so if you'll just tell me which road——'

No! The word screamed inside Saffron's head, cutting through the whirl of confusion and anger like a cold metal blade, so that suddenly she could think again, her short-circuited brain-cells beginning to make connections—and the link she could see between her own comment about buying her for the cost of a dinner and his insulting, 'If you'll just tell me your terms...' of earlier that day, made her blood boil.

'I'm not going anywhere with you! Stop the car! Damn you—I said stop!'

CHAPTER FOUR

FOR a terrifying moment she thought he wasn't going to do as she said, and just as she was nerving herself for desperate action—though quite what, she had no idea—Niall shrugged indifferently, and, with a swift glance in the mirror, steered the powerful car to a safe position at the kerb.

It had barely come to a halt when Saffron wrenched at the door, only to find that, to her intense frustration, the handle remained stubbornly immovable, resisting all her efforts.

'Open this!' she flung at Niall, brown eyes flashing fire.

'Calm down. Can't we talk about this like rational human beings?' His tone was one that a vet might use to soothe a highly-strung horse, but it had exactly the opposite effect on her.

'There's nothing to talk about! I'm not going anywhere with you, so open this door!'

'It's locked, and it's going to stay locked until you're prepared to discuss things like a reasonable——'

'There is nothing to discuss! And how you dare use the word *reasonable* in the context of what you've done——'

'What have I done?' Niall's immovable calm was infuriating. 'No—tell me,' he went on at her angrily wordless exclamation. 'Just what is it that has so offended you? I've made it obvious that I find you attractive—so much so that I wanted to spend some time alone with you—is there anything wrong with that?'

45

Put that way, it sounded perfectly reasonable, Saffron had to admit, though it ignored the high-handed way he had behaved.

'Oh, perhaps I should have *asked* if you felt the same way, but usually my instincts on such things are pretty reliable. If I apologise, will that help matters? I *am* sorry if I behaved like a—what did you call it?—a primitive Neanderthal. I didn't plan on using caveman tactics.'

When he paused, obviously waiting for some response, Saffron could only manage an incomprehensible murmur, a sound halfway between a growl of rejection and a mumbled acceptance of his apology. What he had said was all very well, but it didn't do anything to ease nerves made tight with suspicion or erase the memory of the way he had treated her in the MD's office that morning. But when his mouth quirked up at the corners like that, his eyes glinting with humour in the light of the streetlamp, his whole face changed, that smile making his expression much more appealing—dangerously so for her peace of mind.

'So now will you let me drive you home?'

Still not fully convinced, Saffron regarded him in mutinous silence, so that he sighed his exasperation, raking an impatient hand through the sleek darkness of his hair.

'You're determined not to make this easy for me.'

'Then why don't you just let me get out and make my own way home?'

She had little hope that he would give in that easily, and of course he didn't.

'At this time of night? You must be joking.'

'I'm perfectly capable of looking after myself.' She wouldn't let herself think of the fact that the buses stopped at ten and she doubted if she had enough cash in her purse for a taxi-fare.

'I'm sure you are. You seem lke one very independent lady to me.'

Saffron wasn't quite sure why that comment stung so sharply. Possibly it had something to do with the sardonic emphasis he gave it, seeming to communicate the fact that her independence was not a characteristic that appealed. What she liked even less was the way he shook his head, adamantly rejecting her hopeful suggestion.

'I'll give you a choice,' he said. 'Either you give me directions to your home now——' That disturbing smile resurfaced at the sight of Saffron's suspicious expression.

'Or——?' she prompted stubbornly, refusing to let herself be swayed by the softening effect it had on his hard-featured face.

'Or I'll take you back to my hotel and we'll talk it out there,' he finished blithely.

Which, of course, left her with no choice at all, as he knew only too well. The prospect of being on Niall's own territory, so to speak—which smacked very much of putting her head at least into the lion's den if not actually into the lion's mouth—was not one she relished at all.

'All right, then——'

Her voice revealed her reluctance, but she had been left with no alternative. There was only one comfort to be drawn from all this, she reflected as she gave the first set of directions. She'd be willing to bet that Niall hadn't bargained for her living so far out of town. He had probably thought that she had a flat in Kirkham itself, and so would not be anticipating the long drive through the centre and out the other side.

If she had expected any complaint when he realised what was happening, she was disappointed. Apart from her instructions, the drive was continued in complete silence, Niall only revealing his feelings when she directed him on to the York road and told him to follow it for a couple of miles by another of those swift, sidelong glances, this one touched with faint suspicion. Meeting it head-on, Saffron smiled back at him with blithe innocence.

'You wanted to drive me home,' she said sweetly. 'Surely you're not having second thoughts?'

'Not at all—after all, the idea was to spend some time on my own with you.'

Which was guaranteed to drive all sense of triumph from her mind, bringing her up sharply against the fact that, now that they had left the lights of the town behind them, the road was very dark and deserted and she was in the company of a man who had propositioned her in no uncertain terms that morning. Hastily Saffron abandoned a half-formed plan of sending Niall the long way round, opting instead for the quicker route through the village. The satisfaction she might have obtained from giving him an unnecessarily long journey didn't outweigh the more practical concern of ensuring she got home safely.

'Turn right here——'

As she spoke she lifted her hand, meaning simply to indicate the correct direction, but the movement made her fingers brush against the hard strength of his arm beneath the fine material of his suit jacket. Immediately she felt as if she had touched a live electric wire, a shock of several hundred volts shooting through her hand and making her snatch it back hastily, shrinking down into her seat.

At first she thought that Niall hadn't noticed her reaction, but once he had negotiated the sharp turn and they were travelling along the straight road again he said quietly, 'There's no need to panic—I'm not an axe-murderer.'

'I never thought you were!' Saffron retorted, and then, to cover the revealing quaver in her voice, added with what she hoped was a convincing display of airy insouciance, 'And I'm not worried!'

'Then you should be,' Niall returned sharply, metaphorically snatching the rug from under her feet. 'Do you make a habit of getting into cars with men you don't know?'

'No, I do not make a "habit" of it!'

Strangely, it was the undercurrent of anger in his voice that made her feel better about the situation. She was profoundly relieved to find that he had put her nervous response down to fear. If he had known the real way she was feeling—with every nerve seemingly heightened, quiveringly aware of the lean power of his body so close to hers, of that faintly musky scent tantalising her nostrils, setting up a twisting, disturbing response deep inside her——his reaction might have been very different.

'And may I remind you that—one—you didn't exactly give me much choice about coming with you, and—two—when I got into the car, Owen was with me.'

'A great deal of help he'd have been if you'd needed him,' Niall returned drily.

'And whose fault was that?'

'Saffron—I did not pour the damn wine down his throat. I simply provided the opportunity for him to drink it if he chose. He could have stopped me at any time—he only had to refuse—to say no...'

His pause was perfectly timed, just long enough to alert her to the fact that something more was to follow, something significant enough to have her sitting tensely upright, her eyes on his shadowed face.

'As do you.'

'I wasn't aware of the fact that I'd said yes to anything!' Saffron snapped, and was thoroughly disconcerted to hear the soft, warm sound of his laughter.

'Oh, Saffron, you didn't have to *say* that. Everything about you—every look, every bit of body language—has already said it for you.'

Which was guaranteed to drive every ounce of fight from her in the same way that a blow to her chest would have left her breathless and gasping for air. But even through the reeling sense of confusion she registered, with a small flare of pleasure, just how attractive her name sounded when he spoke it in that warm, amused voice that turned the syllables into something close to a sensual caress, making her feel that she had never heard it before in her life. How much more caressing would it sound if it was whispered in more intimate surroundings, when that low, husky voice murmured words of love?

'So, where do we go from here?'

'Nowhere!'

Dragged from the sensual little dream into which her wanton thoughts had taken her, Saffron snapped out the word in an instinctively defensive response, and was shocked into total alertness, her heart pounding, as Niall suddenly swung the car to the side of the road and slammed on the brakes. With the sound of the engine shut off the country lane seemed very silent, and threateningly dark and deserted, the man beside her very big and powerful.

'Wh-what are you doing? Why have we stopped?'

'You tell me.' The look Niall turned on her was worryingly enigmatic, just a flash of those silvery eyes in the moonlight, revealing nothing. 'You're the navigator—I'm the one who doesn't know my way around.'

'You——!'

Saffron almost choked on her exclamation of disbelief.

'I doubt if you've ever been unsure of where you're going in your entire life. You must have been born knowing exactly which path you were going to fol-low——'

No, not follow—which path he would *take*, she amended privately. Niall was one of life's takers, never a follower.

'But not now. Well, sweetheart?' That rich voice had softened even more, whispering over her sensitised nerves. 'Why *have* we stopped?'

'Because you——'

Even in the darkness she could sense the smile that curled the corners of his mouth and knew that his amusement was at her expense. Slowly the haze of confusion receded and a degree of logical thinking returned as she looked around her with new clarity, seeing just ahead of them the crossroads with its three possible choices of route. Where do we go from here?

'Oh!' Once more she was grateful that the shadows hid the fiery colour in her cheeks as she realised her mistake.

But it seemed that Niall could sense that too, was intuitively aware of her embarrassment and the thoughts that had created it.

'Oh, Saffron—what *were* you thinking? Did you really imagine that seduction was what I had in mind? That I'd stopped the car in order to have my wicked way with you? I'm thirty-two, sweetheart . . .'

The amusement in his voice had deepened into something so dangerously close to laughter that it was threatening to her self-control.

'A little too old to be making out in cars. But, of course, you're not——'

'I'm twenty-five!'

Tension made her voice tight. If he was going to pounce, why didn't he do it? At least then she would have something to react against.

But pouncing seemed to be the last thing on Niall's mind. Far from being a fiercely predatory jungle cat, now he seemed instead like a sleepily satisfied tiger, one that was content to lie back lazily and watch his potential prey thrash itself into a frenzy of fear, without any inclination to hunt. So, had she read all the signals wrong? Had she misinterpreted what was in fact just a simple offer of help? But how could anyone misinterpret, 'If you tell me your terms...' and the way he had got Owen drunk?

'And I'm not your sweetheart!'

Privately she cursed the shake in her voice, knowing it would not go unnoticed—and of course it didn't.

'What's wrong, honey?'

The soft voice was deceptively solicitous, and as he spoke he leaned even closer, so that Saffron had to close her eyes against the sensual assault created by the mixture of that subtle aftershave with the clean male scent of his body. He was so near that she could almost feel the heat of his skin through the barrier of their clothes.

'Are you disappointed that the only reason I stopped was that I didn't know which way to go—to reach your house, I mean?'

It was a snake-charmer's voice, Saffron thought desperately, one that would hypnotise and control even the most dangerous of reptiles, and the mocking humour behind the deliberate double meaning only added to her feeling of losing control. As if in response to that voice, her own private serpent of need was waking once more deep inside her, stretching, uncoiling...

He was so close that he was almost touching her, and yet not quite. He was so near and yet so far, and she

was so intensely physically aware of the latent power of
that lean, male body that it came as a sudden shock to
realise that, apart from that disturbing handshake, he
had never really touched her. It didn't seem like that.
Instead, she felt so sensitive to every move he made, to
the soft sound of his breathing, the strong beat of his
heart, that it was as if he actually held her imprisoned
in a confining grip, as if his voice and eyes had been
fine metal strands that had spun an unbreakable web to
hold her.

'*Are* you disappointed? Because I'll tell you a secret—
so am I. It seems a terrible pity to waste such a perfect
opportunity——'

Through ears sensitised by the fact that she couldn't
see, Saffron heard Niall's indrawn breath, soft as a
caress, and sensed almost physically the movement of
his gaze down to her lips. But she didn't dare to open
her eyes, knowing that if she did so she would not be
able to resist the growing need to reach out and touch
him, to feel the warm strength of the real man beneath
those sophisticated clothes, and a faint whimper of
protest escaped her.

'A terrible pity!'

The sudden change in his tone alerted her, her eyes
flying open, her body poised for flight, as he flung his
safety-belt aside and gathered her into his arms, his
mouth coming down on her.

His gentleness was totally unexpected. If he had been
forceful, demanding, if his kiss had had anything of the
blatant sensuality of his tone, then she would have pan-
icked and resisted, fighting hard to be free. But this was
so unlike the tiger's pounce that she had anticipated.
This was a slow seduction of her senses, a softly enticing
awakening that seemed to draw her soul from her body,
making her head swim and every inch of her skin start

to glow as if the cool light of the moon had suddenly changed, bathing her instead in the heat of a midday sun.

The problem was that her nerves were already awake, needing no gentle encouragement to rouse the passionate fires that were smouldering within her, and before she knew quite what was happening she was responding fiercely, kissing him back with a strength and an intensity that she would never have believed herself capable of. The reaction along every inch of her body and inside her head felt like the eruption of a volcano or the shattering of a meteor falling from the heavens, the touch of Niall's hands leaving a fiery trail like that of a shooting star blazing across the sky.

The last time she had seen such an explosive display of light and brilliance had been years ago when, during a family bonfire display, one of her sisters had accidentally dropped a burning sparkler into the box of fireworks and everything had been set alight at once. But these pyrotechnics were only in her mind, flaring and sparking with a dazzling intensity that made her feel as if *she* was a keg of gunpowder to which Niall had held a lighted torch.

She didn't know how much time had passed before Niall drew back, lifting his head and looking into her eyes, his own expression unseen and unreadable in the darkness. His sigh was a sensuous sound, one of pleasure and contentment, and yet communicated only too clearly the hunger that had not been appeased but stimulated by their closeness, their passionate caresses, so that she knew without a word being spoken that his appetite had been sharpened rather than dulled by the taste he had had of what he wanted.

For a long, silent moment he held her gaze, his pale eyes gleaming in the moonlight, making her think fearfully of the hunting jungle cat to which she had likened him earlier. Then, his movements slow and almost dreamy, he trailed the backs of his fingers down the side of her cheek before lifting the same hand and pushing it roughly through the smooth blackness of his hair.

'Like I said, sweetheart,' he said, in a voice that was low and slightly hoarse, as if his throat was suddenly painfully dry, 'where do we go from here?'

Her senses were still reeling, her pulse throbbing, her body humming like a violin string that had been plucked, but through it all, like a cold, sneaking trickle of icy water, ran the sense of danger that simply being with this man created, the need to act for her own self-preservation shining a cold, rational light into the muddied pool of her thoughts.

'Straight on at the crossroads and take the first turning on the left—it's the fourth house down.'

She refused to let herself be disturbed by the way his head snapped back, his hands dropping from her arms. She could sense the mental distance he had put between them almost as strongly as if it had been a physical one—which in another moment it was, as Niall moved back into the driver's seat, twisting the key in the ignition and revving the engine with an unnecessary violence that spoke more clearly than words of his state of mind.

'First on the left?' he said, and she could only nod in painful silence, the cold harshness of his tone striking her like a physical blow.

Only now, as her body reacted to the loss of his physical warmth, did the chilling sense of losing something very important begin to creep over her, making her feel miserably bereft and unhappy. Without the brilliant explosions of delight his touch had triggered off in her mind, her spirits sank to a despondent low, her eyes unfocused as she stared unseeingly out at the darkened countryside.

But those explosions had been just illusions, as transient and pointless as the momentary brilliance of a firework display that lit up the sky for a few seconds and just as quickly burned itself out. Niall had made it only too plain that he was attracted to her—but that was all. She was something he had wanted and, as he had said, if he wanted something he went for it—and when he tired of it he walked away without a backward glance. She would do well to remember that.

'This the one?'

'Yes——'

Her fingers were already on the handle, waiting for him to release the lock on the door, as he drew the car up by the kerb. Niall studied her cottage in silence for a moment.

'I never expected you to live in a place like this—it looks like a doll's house.'

'It is tiny.' Saffron was relieved to find that her voice was reasonably even and relaxed. 'But that's the way I like it—at least it's all my own; I don't have to share with anyone.'

As soon as the words were out she bit down hard on her lower lip, cursing herself for giving away that vital fact. Luckily, at that moment the handle moved and the door swung open.

'I won't keep you any longer,' she said hastily, trying to sound as casual as possible. 'Thanks for the lift—will you be able to find your way back to town?'

'Oh, I'm sure I can remember the route,' Niall murmured drily. 'Your instructions were clear enough.'

'Well, goodnight...' Saffron decided that discretion was the better part of valour, that it was wisest to ignore that double-edged remark. 'And thanks again.'

She was out of the car and straightening up when Niall moved, leaning across the seat towards her.

'No chance of a cup of coffee?'

Just for a second the appeal of his voice, that smile, almost weakened her, but common sense murmured a hasty warning and she shook her head.

'No—it's late, and I have a job to go to in the morning.'

'Then, what about——?'

'Niall,' she said, emboldened by the fact that it would take him far longer to get out of the car and come round to her than it would for her to run to her house and slam the door against him if it was necessary, 'what part of "no" did you not understand?'

That, and the coolness of her tone, got through to him, and she saw a dark scowl cross his face.

'The word I understand perfectly,' he declared harshly. 'What I can't get my head round is why you're using it when you don't really mean it.'

Then, as she gasped in shock and fury at the arrogance of his words, he shrugged his broad shoulders dismissively and shook his dark head.

'But you did, and so I'll just have to accept that you obviously don't know your own mind as well as I do mine. All right, Saffron—I can wait. Off you go to your little doll's house and your lonely bed. You never know—perhaps you'll dream of me.'

'Never!' Saffron couldn't believe what she was hearing. 'I could never dream of you—and if I did, believe me, it would be a nightmare!'

His smile was like something out of that nightmare, cold and hard and totally humourless, a travesty of the gesture of warmth it was supposed to be.

'Which just proves my point. Forgive me if I don't believe you, sweet Saffron—one of these days I'll show you exactly why.'

'Not if I see you first!' Saffron declared, slamming the door with a violence that gave her intense satisfaction.

But that was as far as her courage went. Not daring to look at his face to see how he had taken her response, for fear that she might discover that he was actually getting out of the car, she headed for her cottage as quickly as her legs would carry her, wrenching the door open and dashing inside, leaning back against the solid wood with a sigh of relief only after she had secured the lock and pushed the two strong bolts home.

Even then, with solid wood between herself and any intruder, she found that her heart was racing painfully, setting a pulse throbbing in her throat so that she could hardly breathe. It was only when she heard the car's powerful engine roar and the tyres squeal as he drove away that she finally managed to make her way into her tiny living-room, where she sank down on the settee, weak with reaction, her legs unable to support her any more.

CHAPTER FIVE

'WELL, come on.' Kate's voice was tinged with barely-controlled impatience. 'Put me out of my misery!'

'Mmm?'

Saffron lifted her head, frowning her confusion. She had been trying to work on the weekly laundry list, but if the truth was told she hadn't been able to read a word on the page, the image of a sleek, dark head and pale, steely eyes dancing before her instead.

'What do you want to know?'

'What do I——?' Kate rolled her eyes expressively. 'Isn't it obvious? Just what happened between you and Owen yesterday?'

'Owen?'

'Yes, Owen—the man to whom you were going to give your all just twenty-four hours ago. Was he impressed by the scarlet siren outfit?'

The laughter in Kate's voice grated over Saffron's tightly strung nerves, and abruptly she turned away, shuffling through the papers in an attempt to hide the burning colour she knew was rising in her face.

'He wasn't there,' she said abruptly, praying that Kate would ask no further questions, but the other girl was not so easily deterred.

'But you saw him last night? And?' she prompted at Saffron's silent nod.

'And he had a bit too much to drink. As a matter of fact, he got decidedly tipsy.'

'Owen!' Kate exclaimed in mock horror. 'Mrs Richards' perfect son! So, of course that meant you had no chance to talk things over—or take any action?'

Once more those exaggeratedly raised blonde eyebrows left Saffron in no doubt as to just what action her friend meant.

'That's not a consideration any more.'

That was one definite decision she had reached last night, as she had tossed and turned restlessly until just before dawn when she had finally fallen into a shallow and unrefreshing sleep.

'I think perhaps I'm not the commitment type after all.'

'Why ever not? How can you have changed so completely in just twenty-four hours?'

Which was just the question that had kept Saffron awake late into the night, though not quite in the context in which Kate had meant it. Just how could she, who had always believed in taking things very steadily where relationships were concerned, have found herself responding to Niall Forrester's kisses with such—such enthusiasm? Her mind flinched away from the more accurate word—passion.

Looking back at the girl who had been in Niall's arms, she couldn't recognise herself in the uninhibited, wanton creature she had become, and in the cold light of day she had been forced to admit that her reaction to him later, her forceful rejection of any further overtures on his part, had really been a form of panic at the thought of how she could have changed so much, so quickly, and as a result she had run away from the man who had been the cause of that change.

'I——' she began, but was interrupted by the ringing of the doorbell downstairs.

'I'll go!'

Kate disappeared down the steps that led to the door into the street, leaving Saffron breathing a silent prayer of gratitude for her escape. She didn't know how she would have answered Kate's question if she had had to.

'Well, now, look at this!' Her friend reappeared in the doorway, a rather smug smile on her face. 'Owen must be feeling very guilty about last night.'

'Those are for me?'

Saffron held out her arms to receive the bouquet of roses, her expression bewildered.

'This isn't at all like Owen. But they are gorgeous.'

'Beautiful! And there's a card—what does it say?'

'Hang on—let me open it! It's——Oh!'

The pleasure faded swiftly from Saffron's face, her heart lurching painfully as she saw the words inscribed on the white card in strong black letters—handwriting that was nothing like Owen's small, precise neatness.

'What is it?'

Curiosity overcoming her, Kate peered over Saffron's shoulder and read the inscription out loud.

'"As soon as I saw these, I thought of you. N. F." Not Owen, then?'

Of course not Owen. Saffron knew that she should have realised that from the first. Owen had never bought her flowers in all the time they had been together.

But she should have known. For one thing, the colour of the glorious flowers should have given her a clue. They were the same rich, glowing scarlet as the silk basque and suspender belt Kate had described as the siren's outfit.

'Who's N. F.?'

She had known that the question must come, and was partially prepared for it.

'Niall Forrester.' To her relief, she was able to say the name without revealing the way her nerves twisted into tight, painful knots at the thought of him. 'A business acquaintance of Owen's. We had dinner with him last night.'

'Was that when Owen blotted his copybook by getting drunk?'

Saffron bit back a groan of despair as she looked into her friend's green eyes, bright with interest, behind which she could almost hear the other girl's brain ticking over, adding two and two together...

'So he wasn't fit to drive...?'

'And, yes, Mr Forrester gave me a lift home—but don't read anything into that,' she added hastily as the gleam in her friend's eyes brightened. 'It was just a polite gesture, nothing more.'

'So why is he sending you flowers?'

'I don't know.'

And that was the honest truth. After the way she had left him last night, the anger she had seen in his face, the cold dismissal in the words he had flung at her, she would have thought that Niall was more likely to want to put her out of his mind for good. But then a memory slid into her mind, the echo of that coolly drawling voice saying, 'I can wait...'

But how had he known to send flowers here instead of to the cottage? How had he found out where she worked? The thought of him asking questions, probing into her life, made a sensation like the trail of icy wet footprints slide slowly down her spine.

'I suppose——'

She wasn't at all sure how she would have gone on if she hadn't been rescued once more by the sound of the bell.

'Now who's this?'

'Let me see to the door while you put those flowers in water,' Kate said obligingly. She was part-way down the stairs when her curiosity got too much to bear. 'And what's he like, this Niall Forrester?'

'Oh, you know——' Saffron aimed for airy insouciance '—a real businessman.' She raised her voice to carry down the stairwell. 'Smooth as silk and oily with it, with nothing to recommend him but his money—boring as hell. *Ow*!'

She broke off on a cry of pain as a sharp thorn caught her thumb through the cellophane wrapping and pricked it savagely. If she had been superstitious, Saffron thought wryly, watching the bright red bead of blood on the tip of her injured finger, she might actually believe that the tiny wound was an act of fate—punishment for lying through her teeth in her description of Niall. But she had had to squash Kate's curiosity once and for all.

As she put her thumb to her mouth to soothe the sharp sting she heard her friend's footsteps mounting the stairs again.

'Who was it?' she asked around her injured finger, and just had time to take in her friend's expression, the look of barely subdued excitement combined with a hint of concern, before her eyes went to the tall, dark figure of the man who stood behind Kate. An uncontrollable groan of reaction escaped her.

'It's Mr Forrester,' Kate announced, the look in her eyes finishing her statement with the unspoken comment, And he's *not* boring! without a word having to be spoken.

For a couple of uncomfortable seconds the room actually seemed to swing round Saffron, making her take a step backwards to lean against the desk for support. Her mind buzzed with questions, wondering frantically just how Niall had found out where she worked and, even more disturbing, just how much of her foolish, unthinking comment he had heard. The door had been closed, but she had raised her voice quite considerably to make sure that it carried far enough to reach Kate.

'Good morning, Saffron.'

Niall's voice was cool and easy, no hint of any strong emotion rufling its smooth surface.

'You got the roses, I see.'

Saffron managed a vague murmur that sounded like agreement, astonishment depriving her of the ability to speak. This wasn't Niall Forrester! At least, he wasn't the man she had had dinner with last night or—her breath caught painfully in her chest—the one she had encountered in the MD's office yesterday morning. The sleek, expensive suit had gone, to be replaced by a well-worn leather jacket, white heavy cotton shirt and a pair of denim jeans so tight and clinging they were positively X-rated. With his black hair blown on to his forehead by the same wind that had brought a glow of colour into his cheeks, he looked vitally alive and potently male, the aura of success and money that surrounded him, even in the very casual clothes, enhancing his undeniable, forceful physical attraction.

As on the previous night, Saffron found herself thinking unnervingly of the similarities between Niall and a wild jungle cat. His sleek appearance was belied by a hint of wildness, an untameable quality that she knew some women would find totally irresistible. Certainly Kate was impressed, if the sparkle in her wide green eyes and the way she could hardly take them off him was anything to go by.

'I hope you like them.'

'I——'

With an effort Saffron clasped her mouth shut on the enthusiastic response that had almost escaped her. Only a few moments before, she had been wondering just why Niall would send her flowers, but of course the answer

was obvious. 'When I see what I want, I go for it——'
Clearly he hadn't taken her refusal of last night as
seriously meant. Just what did she have to do to convince him? She had no desire to end up as just one of
those things he ultimately walked away from without a
backward glance.

'The flowers? They were all right.'

It was a struggle to ignore the way Kate's eyebrows
flew upwards in an expression of frank amazement at
her swift about-turn from her earlier enthusiasm, and
she had to look away hastily, praying that Niall hadn't
seen the other girl's reaction.

'But, really, red roses are such a cliché, don't you
think?'

Niall's smile was a slow, dangerous curling of his sensuous mouth, one that matched the steel-grey ice of his
eyes in its lack of warmth.

'Ah, but then I wasn't thinking of any supposed sym-
bolic meaning that tradition has given them. It was
something else that attracted me. Didn't you read my
note?'

The grey eyes were suddenly smoky, worryingly so, as
his voice softened enticingly, and they drew her gaze once
more, holding it in the same mesmeric spell that he had
managed to weave around her the night before.

'I'll just sort these out——'

With superb tact, Kate picked up a sheaf of papers
from the desk and left the room, heading for the kitchen
below, but neither Saffron nor Niall saw her go.

'When I saw them, I knew I had to buy them for
you...'

Reaching out, he took the bouquet from Saffron's
unresisting grasp and with a neat, efficient movement
drew a single perfect bloom from the bunch.

'I knew how wonderful they would look against your skin.'

The rose brushed her cheek softly, its velvety petals sliding over her skin in a delicate caress that sent a shiver of sensual awareness sliding down her spine. His smile showing his recognition of her response, Niall let the flower trail gently downwards over the pale blue linen of her suit, the white blouse, coming to rest at the point of the deep V-neck, its rich colour startling against her pale skin.

'As they do...' His voice had dropped to a husky whisper.

For a moment Saffron shut her eyes, swallowing hard. Her mind screamed a furious rejection of the suggestive position of the scarlet flower, resting just at the point where her breasts curved softly. But her lids flew open again at the realisation that her temporary blindness only intensified the sensual enticement created by the combination of that low, caressing voice, the delicate touch of the rose's petals and its heady, musky perfume.

Her heart was racing, her mouth dry, and she knew that, under the light pressure of the delicate flower, her breasts rose and fell jerkily with her quickened breathing.

'Yes, well——'

With an abrupt movement she snatched the rose away, refusing to let herself feel any guilt or regret when her rough action snapped the thin stem, breaking it, so that she was left with only the blossom in her hand.

'Roses really aren't my favourite flower.'

In a disdainful gesture she dropped the broken flower-head into the wastepaper bin and moved to seat herself in the swivel chair behind her desk. She felt happier with the solid wood between them, though her composure was severely threatened by the way that Niall immediately took several steps forward, the movement bringing him to stand opposite her, his imposing height emphasised by her position in the chair, so that he seemed to be towering over her. She refused to let herself feel threatened.

'Well, perhaps you'll be more pleased to see these——'

She hadn't noticed the carrier bag in his hand, but as soon as he deposited it on the polished wood of her desk she knew just what it must contain.

'The shoes—how thoughtful.' Her tone dripped a deliberate honeyed sweetness that only a blind fool would take as being sincere. 'Kate will be so pleased to get them back——'

'Kate?'

To her annoyance he didn't look in the least disconcerted. There was even a touch of amusement in the single word, a faint curl at the corners of his mouth.

'You didn't really think they were mine, did you? They wouldn't exactly go with what I'm wearing——'

It wasn't just the shoes that she wanted him to know were not hers, but the image of the woman who had worn them. She knew that the picture she presented now, with her dark hair pinned up in a neat coil at the nape of her neck, wearing the severely tailored suit and blouse, was one of controlled, businesslike efficiency, light-years away from the scarlet-clad siren he had first set eyes on.

'Hardly.' Disconcertingly, the laughter was more pronounced now. 'But then you wouldn't be the first woman to conceal her true self under a carefully restrained exterior.'

The smile grew, becoming a wicked grin that was mirrored in the glinting grey eyes.

'I learned very early on not to judge a woman's character by her clothes but by what she wears beneath them.'

'And I suppose that you've tested out that theory on innumerable occasions?'

'Hardly innumerable—that would be totally irresponsible. But, yes, I've evidence to support the premise.'

'Well, in my case, I'm afraid your theory doesn't hold water—though I suppose you would say that makes me the exception that proves the rule.'

She was going to regret provoking him. She knew that as she saw the wicked glint in his eye brighten perceptibly.

'On the contrary. With you, I'm forced to wonder just what makes you so determined to deny your true self by——'

'Don't you really mean that I'm denying you?' Saffron snapped acidly.

Infuriatingly, her barbed dart seemed to bounce ineffectually off his thick skin.

'Not at all. I've told you—I'm perfectly prepared to wait until you come to your senses.'

'Then you'll wait till hell freezes over!'

'Oh, I don't think so——'

Too bemused by Niall's smooth-toned arrogance to think of a suitably crushing retort, Saffron was infinitely relieved when their conversation was interrupted at just that moment by the shrill summons of the phone. She was even happier to discover that the identity of the caller meant that she had to call for Kate, who reappeared swiftly, hurrying to answer.

The slight pause had given her the opportunity to collect her thoughts, restore some degree of composure.

'So, tell me, Mr Forrester——' Deliberately she emphasised the formality of her use of his surname, hoping it would distance her from him mentally as well as her position behind the desk did physically. 'What can we do for you?'

Her glance in the direction of her friend made it plain that Kate was included in the question every bit as much as herself, that 'we' having been used as meaningfully as the 'Mr Forrester', as was the gesture she now made towards the other girl, who had now finished her conversation and was replacing the receiver.

'I'm sorry—this is my partner, Kate Macallinden. She runs A Movable Feast with me.'

'Miss Macallinden——' Kate was treated to the sort of smile that, if it had been an electric light, would have had to be measured in megawatts, and Saffron saw her friend actually step back in reaction to its stunning brilliance.

'Kate, this is Niall Forrester. His company is taking over Richards' Rockets.'

The sudden recollection of that silkily emphasised 'possibly' on the previous night made her stumble over her words. He had never put any such qualifying terms on his insolent declaration that she was exactly what he had been looking for.

'Now—how can we help you?'

'That really rather depends on exactly what sort of services you're willing to provide,' Niall returned smoothly, and, having floored her with the deliberate double meaning, he went on with a smile, 'But, after last night, I think we can dispense with the formality of surnames, don't you?'

Which was guaranteed to make Kate even more curious, Saffron reflected furiously, refusing even to look at her friend, knowing only too well the intrigued message her expressive eyes would be telegraphing— wanting to know just what Niall had meant by 'after last night'.

'A Movable Feast is a catering company——'

Furious with herself for having fallen into his trap, she launched into her business speech, deciding that her professional persona was the best one to hide behind at this particular moment. At least it kept the topic of conversation to strictly impersonal matters—though Niall seemed capable of twisting anything round to mean something else entirely!

'We can provide food for any sort of function, formal or informal—a child's birthday party—a twenty-first— a picnic at the races—even——' she couldn't stop the hopeful note from creeping into her voice '—business lunches or meals for staff attending conferences.'

Perhaps he *was* looking for someone to offer to take on a contract for staff meals at Richards' Rockets. With something like that under her belt, she wouldn't need to worry about money quite so much.

'You just name the occasion and we'll do the rest. We provide sample menus for you to choose from—all the china and cutlery——'

Niall looked slightly bemused at her enthusiasm.

'I didn't realise you were quite such a forceful businesswoman.'

'Why—did you think that I was merely a decorative accessory to Owen?' Anger sparked at the thought. 'Just an attractive adornment, the traditional requirement of a successful businessman, a bimbo without a brain in my head?'

The mocking question implied by the way one dark eyebrow drifted slowly upwards stopped her dead in mid-tirade. After all, their first meeting was hardly likely to have given him any other impression.

'You hardly gave me a chance to come to any conclusion—you were so damn determined I should talk to Richards,' he retorted. 'But, if I do decide to spend some time in Kirkham, perhaps I might be able to use your company.'

'Our rates are very competitive.' Saffron made no attempt to hide her keenness. 'And I'm sure you'll find that, although we're only a small establishment, we can match the very best. What exactly was it that you had in mind?'

'A special night with a special lady?' Niall murmured, with a wicked smile that made her heart lurch painfully. 'Perhaps we could discuss the details over lunch?'

'Lunch?'

Saffron schooled her face into something that approximated polite disappointment. If he really planned to use their services, it would be a terrible mistake to alienate him completely, but after that dig there was no way she would consider eating with him.

'I think I'm busy—another client——'

'Not for lunch.' Either Kate was blithely unaware of Saffron's attempt to wriggle out of the invitation or she was determined to ignore it. 'Mr Robinson won't be here until after two.'

'Then, lunch it is.' Niall was swift to seize on the opportunity she had given him. 'I'll collect you at twelve-thirty.'

And before she had time to protest, or think of a possible excuse, he had strolled from the room and could be heard running lightly down the stairs. If she had been alone, Saffron would have screamed or stamped her foot in rage at the way he had outmanoeuvred her, but she had to be content with screwing up a piece of paper and flinging it furiously into the bin.

Kate, however, felt no such restraint.

'Wow!' she exclaimed dramatically. 'Now I see why Owen's in the doghouse!'

'Don't be silly!' Saffron snapped. 'Niall Forrester has nothing to do with it.'

The look her friend turned on her was frankly sceptical.

'Oh, doesn't he?' she said. 'Well, that's not the way it appears to me.'

'It's just a business lunch, Kate. After all, we desperately need his custom.'

But, even as she spoke them, Saffron had to admit that, coming from anyone else, she wouldn't have found her words at all convincing. And, to judge by Kate's smile, neither did she.

CHAPTER SIX

'SO, WHEN exactly are you planning this special meal?'

The only way to play this, Saffron had decided, was absolutely straight, pretending that those words meant nothing to her other than the possibility of some much-needed business.

'I'm not sure.'

Niall shrugged broad shoulders under the crisp cotton of his shirt. For the first time that year the wintry weather had improved slightly, finally becoming more like May, and he had discarded the leather jacket as they sat outside the riverside pub he had driven her to, slinging it over the back of his chair and lounging back to enjoy the warmth of the sun.

'I told you, I haven't thought of the details yet.'

'Well, perhaps you'd like to think about them now.'

It was a struggle to be strictly businesslike. She had to force herself to ignore the way the sunlight caught on the glossy blackness of his hair, highlighting its sheen, the way it made those pale eyes gleam like burnished silver, cool against the warm tinge of his skin. Those long legs in the worn denim were stretched out in front of him, dangerously close to her own slim ones, and she moved rather pointedly, earning herself a swift, dark frown.

'Did you want to entertain at home or——'

Her throat closed suddenly at the thought of the implications of Niall 'entertaining' at home, and she reached hastily for her glass of mineral water, swallowing hard to ease the constriction.

'Eat your lunch,' Niall commanded brusquely. 'We can talk about that later.'

'But I *need* to know what you want!'

'Do you?'

The words fell sharply into the silence that had descended as soon as—too late—she realised just what a mistake her own comment had been.

'Do you really want to know, Saffron?' Niall questioned softly, dangerously. 'Because I'll tell you if you like—but you'd better be very sure that that is what you want.'

'Niall!'

It was a croaked protest, too feeble to have any effect. He was determined; she knew that from the set of his features, the sudden smokiness of those formerly clear grey eyes.

'I want *you*, Saffron.'

The words were silkily intent, pitched to reach her ears only, and, as on the previous night, it was suddenly as if they were no longer in a public place, but enclosed in an intimate bubble, shut off from the rest of the world.

'I want you so much that I've gone completely off my head. You're driving me crazy, Saffron——'

'Oh, come on!' she managed shakily. 'You're exaggerating!'

'I told you, I never exaggerate,' he shot back. 'And if you don't believe me you can ring my secretary. Ask her about the meetings she's had to postpone—the appointments she's had to rearrange—the schedule she's probably still struggling to readjust—no doubt cursing me to hell and back as she does it.'

'But why?' Saffron stammered, and earned herself a look of laughing reproach.

'Think about it,' he murmured, holding her shocked, wide-eyed gaze with hypnotic ease once more. 'My secretary thinks I've blown several fuses; my deputy manager will probably never speak to me again; I may have lost a valuable contract, and there's an important meeting I should be at right this minute. But I didn't even consider them when I decided what to do today. I'm where I want to be right now, with the person I want to——'

'Niall,' Saffron interjected hastily, 'you can't——'

'Why can't I?'

'But your company—those people—that contract——'

A nonchalant wave of his hand dismissed her concerns and the needs of his job as totally unimportant.

'They'll always be there, and if not I can replace them. Since you walked into my life yesterday...'

Was it really only the previous day? Saffron wondered shakily. She felt as if she had lived through several lifetimes since then. Barely thirty hours had passed, and yet she knew that she could never take the scattered jigsaw pieces of her life and put them back together in such a way that they would form exactly the same picture as before. That image of her existence was shattered and gone forever.

'...I've only been able to think of one thing—you. Your eyes, your hair, your face——'

His own eyes darkened even more, becoming almost black, with only the tiniest rim of silver at the edges.

'Your body——'

'Please!'

Fiery colour rushed into Saffron's cheeks. It seemed somehow indecent to be sitting like this, in this quiet, sunlit garden, with the subdued chatter of the other people all around them blending with the ripple of the river in the background, hearing words that would be far better suited to the privacy of a bedroom.

'Naturally, I'm flattered—who wouldn't be?—but I can't really believe that a man like you, who holds the reins of a huge corporation in his hands—on whose shoulders rests the responsibility for thousands of jobs—would let those reins drop—would neglect everything—just because—because——' She faltered, unable to complete the sentence.

'Because of you?' he finished for her. 'Believe it. I had planned to go back to London as soon as I'd finished with Richards. I *should* have gone back then, but after you appeared so dramatically in my office yesterday morning I couldn't get you out of my mind. I couldn't leave Kirkham without finding out more about you. The receptionist told me your name, and about your relationship with Owen; Owen's mother told me he was at Le Figaro, so I knew there was a good chance you would be too.'

Owen's mother had told him! So his appearance at the restaurant had not been the appalling coincidence she had believed it to be. And this morning——

'How did you find out where I worked?'

Niall's lips curled in a worrying smile, and once more Saffron felt the same icy footprints creeping down her spine that she had experienced earlier at the thought of him asking questions. She was beginning to feel like a frightened rabbit, running from a very determined and skilful hunter. 'When I see what I want, I go for it.' But when he had got what he wanted and had tired of it, by his own admission, that was when he coldly walked away.

'Mrs Richards again. She gave me the information when I rang this morning to see how her son was faring after last night's indulgence——'

'You rang Owen?' Saffron couldn't disguise her surprise. 'Isn't that a touch hypocritical? I mean, it's rather like some thuggish mugger phoning the hospital to ask about the progress of his latest victim.'

'His mama appreciated my concern. And, yes,' Niall added, deliberately emphasising the dark irony that threaded through his voice, 'he's fine—if a little hungover.'

'I never doubted that he would be.' Saffron refused to let herself be pushed into feeling guilty that she hadn't been the one to enquire about Owen's condition, that it hadn't even crossed her mind.

'And on my way through the town centre I passed a flower shop,' Niall went on, as if her interjection had never happened. 'Those roses were in the window, and as soon as I saw them, naturally I thought of you.'

'Naturally,' Saffron echoed sardonically, refusing to let herself dwell on just what his thoughts would have been.

'I'm sorry you didn't care for them—you must let me know what you prefer so that the next time——'

Saffron couldn't let him go on.

'There isn't going to be a next time. What do I have to do to convince you of that? I told you last night——'

'I know what you *said* last night, but I also know that I don't believe it. I held you in my arms, remember?'

Remember! Could she ever forget it? Once more, Saffron reached for her glass, wanting to ease the sudden heat in her body that had nothing to do with the mild warmth of the sun, but almost immediately reconsidered, setting it down again without taking a sip at the realisation that there was no way she would be able to swallow. She was sure that the water would catch on the tight knot of feelings in her throat, choking her.

'I kissed you. I felt your response. I saw it in your eyes—as I can see it now——'

And before Saffron had time to think, to register just what he had said, he was on his feet and moving round the white-painted wrought-iron table, pulling her to her feet, clasping her tight against his powerful body with one arm while his other hand slid under her chin, lifting her face to his as his mouth swooped downwards.

If his words had been indecent, then his kiss was practically pornographic in its deliberate sensuality. It made Saffron's blood sweep hotly through her veins, her legs giving way beneath her so that she leaned limply against Niall, supported only by his strength. Her soul seemed to be drawn from her body, her head spinning wildly as if she was delirious, and the coiled serpent in the pit of her stomach lifted its head in an act of sharp need.

It was several moments before she became aware of anything other than Niall, the hard power of his body, the warmth of his skin and its intensely personal, musky scent, and only when she was released, blinking hard as if she had been dazzled by a sudden bright light, did she come back to a realisation of just where she was and the interested stares of the other diners.

'Niall!' she whispered in angry reproach. 'People are watching!'

'Let them watch.'

His shrug was a gesture of supreme indifference, and with total composure he simply returned to his seat, refusing to acknowledge the openly fascinated stares of the people around them.

'It's all right for you!' Hastily Saffron sat down too, making sure her back was to their audience. 'You don't have to live here, with these people! Kirkham is a small place——'

'They're just envious.' Niall dismissed her concern. 'And I was right, wasn't I? You did want me to kiss you—it was written all over your face.'

Did he know her better than she knew herself? He must do, because what he had said he'd seen in her face was something she hadn't known she wanted until he had taken her in his arms. Only then had she realised that she needed his kiss so much that she felt she would have died if he hadn't kissed her.

'Just tell me one thing—can Owen make you feel like that?'

'Owen——'

The burning colour left Saffron's face, leaving her looking pale and strained at the thought of what she had almost revealed. She might have come to the conclusion that there was no future for her relationship with Owen, but she could just imagine what interpretation Niall would put on that decision if she let him know about it.

'What about Owen?' She had trouble getting the words out, struggling with the uncomfortable twisting of the nerves in her stomach.

'What about him?' Niall was clearly not pleased with the mention of the other man's name, even though he had been the first to use it.

'*Will* you buy Richards'?'

'I told you—I haven't made my mind up yet.'

Privately, Saffron took leave to doubt any such thing. All she had seen of Niall Forrester left her in no doubt at all that he was a man who made up his mind far more quickly than most.

'There are one or two—considerations—to be taken into account.'

'Considerations?' Saffron echoed hollowly, her thoughts growing even more uncomfortable. 'Is this an attempt to blackmail me into your bed?'

'Blackmail?'

Either Niall was a far better actor than she had realised, or that was genuine confusion that showed in his eyes, making Saffron suddenly a prey to strong second thoughts about her outburst. 'Blackmail?' Niall repeated, and she knew there was no backing down now.

'If I don't sleep with you, then you won't buy Owen's company, is that it? Because, if it is, then you couldn't be more wrong. I don't care if Owen doesn't get the price he wants for the factory, or if he never gets that damn night-club he's been hankering after! So if you think you can use that as a hold over me——'

The words died in her throat as she saw the way Niall's eyes narrowed, the cynical twist to his mouth.

'Dear me, what a vivid imagination you have,' he drawled with sardonic mockery. 'Did you really think I'd stoop so low? I've never had to force any woman into my bed in my life—or use blackmail, which, after all, is the psychological equivalent. And, even if I did, I would never bother to bring Richards into this. You see, I've known right from the start that he wasn't the man for you.'

'What do you mean? You don't know anything about me——'

'Oh, come on, Saffron! Any fool can see that a man who'd turn down an invitation like the one you offered me——' the dark smokiness of his eyes told her only too clearly that he was thinking of the scene in the MD's office '—hasn't enough red blood in his veins to handle a real woman.'

'How do you know that he did?'

'Oh, I know.' His voice was rich with loathsome conviction, a dark triumph that seared over her hyper-sensitive nerves. 'I know frustration when I see it, and you were burning up with it. He turned you down flat—either that or he wasn't even offered what you were offering me.'

'I wasn't——' Saffron began, but he ignored her, continuing with silky ruthlessness.

'Was that it, sweetheart? Did you change your mind?' 'Once I'd set eyes on you?'

God, the man was arrogant beyond belief! She'd give anything to knock him down a peg or two—or three!

'You really have got the biggest ego of any man I ever met! Did you honestly believe that because I met you then suddenly I'd forget all about Owen——?'

Her voice failed her embarrassingly as a ruthless conscience brought her hard up against some harsh facts. Because wasn't it actually strictly true? Didn't Niall's arrogant claim have some real foundation in fact?

And, all the more worrying, what had happened to her own conviction that she was ready for commitment? She had told Kate that that was what had been in her mind, had used it to justify her decision to sleep with Owen—but had that just been sex, pure and simple, all along? Was she, in Niall's crudely blunt terminology, so burningly frustrated by her celibate state that she would turn to any man—to Owen—or——?

Or Niall. The thought slid unwanted into her mind, shocking her like a slap in the face, reminding her of her powerful response to him, her intense physical awareness of his presence. Just to look at him sent a blazing heat rushing through her veins, and when he touched her she fizzed like a firecracker. No, she couldn't be so shallow! Violently she shook her head to drive the disturbing thought from her mind.

'No?' Niall questioned, seeing the betraying movement. 'Is that, no, you didn't change your mind, or no, Owen wasn't offered what I was?'

'I never offered *anything* to you! I thought you were Owen!'

Too late, she realised how bad that sounded, following on from her earlier declaration that she didn't give a damn about Owen. Still, what did it matter? she thought bitterly. Niall obviously thought she was cheap and mercenary enough to sell herself to the highest bidder, and, after the way they had first met, could she really blame him?

'So why didn't you repeat your offer to Owen? Oh, I know you haven't.' Niall went on when Saffron glared at him furiously. 'He complained about how—unforth-coming—you were.'

'He did *what*?' Saffron couldn't believe what she was hearing.

'You actually discussed me with him——!'

'On the contrary—I never said a word. Owen, however, seemed to think I'd want to know all about you.'

And he obviously had been quite open about some very intimate details too! She couldn't believe that she had ever considered any form of commitment to the louse. And as for Niall Forrester—he might claim that he hadn't said anything, but he was clearly prepared to use what he had heard against her!

Suddenly she couldn't bear to remain in his company a moment longer. Pushing back her chair with an ugly scraping noise, she got to her feet in a rush.

'I'd like to get back—I do have an appointment!' she added fiercely when Niall looked pointedly at his watch.

'Fine!' He stood up too, raising his hands in a defensive gesture against her fury, the impact of which was belied by the laughter in those silvery eyes. 'Don't take it out on me just because your boyfriend can't be trusted to be discreet!'

'Discreet is not the word!' Saffron flung at him from between clenched teeth as he turned towards the exit.

'And you didn't have to listen—I've never heard of anything so bloody ungentlemanly and——!'

'Oh, didn't you know?' Niall drawled tauntingly when her anger left her lost for words. 'There weren't exactly too many gentlemen around in Neanderthal times. Which reminds me——'

Abruptly he came to an unexpected halt, but, driven by blind fury, Saffron marched straight past him.

'I said I wanted to get back to work!' she threw over her shoulder, heading for the spot where his car was parked. 'So would you mind getting a move on?'

For one awful moment she thought that her shrewish tone would drive him finally to lose his temper. The sensual mouth compressed to a thin, hard line, his eyes narrowing dangerously, so that she flinched inside, anticipating the coming explosion. But then somehow he seemed to rein in the violence that was simmering inside him as he moved to open the car door for her.

But, once inside the sleek vehicle, he showed no sign of being prepared to start the engine.

'I'm going to be late!'

Niall's response was a second, even more pointed glance at the clock on the dashboard, which showed only too clearly that they had over twenty-five minutes in which to make a journey that had taken no more than ten on the way out.

'I have something to say, and we're not going anywhere until you listen,' he stated, in a tone which brooked no further argument.

CHAPTER SEVEN

SAFFRON'S breath hissed between her teeth in a sound that she hoped was more expressive of her earlier impatience than the sudden twinge of fearful apprehension that gripped her at the way he spoke.

'You really seem to make a habit of this——' she began, then broke off abruptly as he made a sound that was a blend of exasperation and a genuine snort of laughter.

'Only because you drive me to it! It seems to be the only way I can get you to listen to a word I say.'

'That's because I don't want to hear——'

'Oh, yes you do,' he interrupted firmly. 'Because I want to apologise.'

'You——'

Saffron knew she was gaping foolishly, but she just couldn't stop herself. She didn't believe she had heard right. Had Niall really said *apologise*?

'For what?' she asked suspiciously, and to her complete consternation his laughter grew into a genuine grin, that devastating smile lighting his face in a way that made her heart thud dangerously in her chest, making her breathing fast and uneven.

'Don't you ever let up? All right,' he went on hurriedly, when she glared at him threateningly, 'I wanted to say that I'm sorry if I behaved badly last night. Believe it or not, that was one of the reasons I asked you to have lunch with me—so that I could apologise for behaving like a—what was it you called me?—a barbaric Neanderthal?'

'Primitive,' Saffron managed shakily, weakened by that smile. She didn't believe for one moment that Niall actually meant his apology—the big man himself saying he was sorry? No way!

'Yeah, well. I think barbaric was in there somewhere too. You were right, though, I shouldn't have manipulated you like that—or got Owen drunk. I never meant to ride roughshod all over you. From now on I'll always give you the choice—all right?'

'All right.' Saffron nodded shakily, her brain reeling in shock at the sudden change in his behaviour. He had actually sounded sincere, his apology apparently genuine. Whatever had happened to the arrogant, lordly Niall Forrester?

'Forgiven?' he asked softly.

'Apology accepted,' Saffron muttered, not prepared to go quite that far. 'Forgiven' sounded like conceding too much, meeting him more than halfway.

She was startled by Niall's response. His unexpected laughter had a warm, friendly sound that went straight to her heart, easing the angry discomfort that the thought of Owen's behaviour had left behind.

'Still fighting?' he murmured teasingly. 'What is it about me, Saffron, that strikes such sparks off you? You're like one of Owen's damn rockets—light the blue touchpaper and stand well back—you're on an exceptionally short fuse!'

'*I* am?' Saffron exclaimed disbelievingly. That description sounded as if it could be applied far more accurately to Niall himself. 'Ever since I first met you I've felt as if I was in the middle of some huge, uncontrolled firework display, with rockets exploding all over the place and Catherine Wheels whirling—firecrackers sending sparks up into the sky.'

'Really?' Niall's tone was rich with dark satisfaction. 'Well, at least you're prepared to admit that I'm having some effect on you.'

'I didn't say I liked it!' Saffron retorted hastily, realising how much she had given away.

She had been too easily swayed by that smile, his laughter, she told herself. He might have apologised, but only for manipulating her into his car and for getting Owen drunk—not for anything else.'

'But you do—don't you?'

It was that snake-charmer's voice again, slow and softly seductive, coiling round her senses like warm smoke, and his eyes held hers captive. She was incapable of looking away in spite of the urgent commands from her brain. Her throat was suddenly parched and she swallowed nervously, her tongue coming out to moisten painfully dry lips. As it did so, she saw the silvery gaze drop downwards to follow the small revealing movement, and her stomach clenched on a painful spasm of response.

'Don't fight me on this, Saffron,' Niall urged huskily. 'Not any more—because, quite frankly, I won't believe you, and it all seems such a waste of energy.'

'I——' Saffron tried to protest, but he laid a gentle finger over her lips to silence her.

'You admit that since we met there have been fireworks between us, and I know you respond to me physically—most people would be glad enough to start from there——'

'A few kisses!' Saffron protested against his restraining finger, and immediately wished that she hadn't because the feel of the warmth of his skin against her lips, the slightly salty taste of it, sent shockwaves of response shooting along her nerves like tiny, brilliant explosions in a chain reaction that built up to a force of nuclear intensity, so that instinctively she closed her eyes against her reaction, terrified of what she might reveal to his watchful gaze.

'A few kisses...' she heard Niall repeat, his voice a sensual caress in itself. 'That is one hell of an understatement, lady. And those kisses were only the start—let me show you——'

She hadn't the strength to move away—and even if she had found it, she knew she couldn't have found the will to use it. 'Don't fight me,' he had said, and suddenly she didn't know why she had been fighting, or even what she was struggling against.

She *wanted* his kisses, wanted the excitement they lit up inside her. Fireworks, Niall had called it, but it was more than that. It was fireworks and rockets and, above all, like setting a torch to a hot, blazing bonfire that had been standing, already carefully laid, just waiting for one tiny spark to set it flaring. Niall, it seemed, had the necessary match, and all he had to do was touch it to the bone-dry tinder and suddenly she was totally alight, all hesitancy, all reticence melting away in the heat of the need blazing up inside her.

When his lips touched hers she gave a small, wordless moan of delight, her fingers moving up of their own volition to link together under the silky black hair at the nape of his neck, drawing his face down to hers and holding him a willing prisoner. Her body was crushed against his, the hardness of his chest against the soft warmth of her breasts, and she could feel the fierce racing of his heart that echoed her own heightened response, making her writhe in aching frustration.

Niall laughed softly and slid his fingers down her cheek, down over the path that he had traced with the delicate petals of the rose, and down, and down... And this time he didn't allow the silk of her blouse to hinder him, but slipped the tiny buttons from their fastenings with practised ease, sliding warm, strong fingers in to push aside the lacy barrier of her underwear and capture one satiny breast in a tantalisingly gentle grip.

'You see,' he whispered in her ear, his breath warm against her cheek, his thumb moving teasingly over the roused nipple as she murmured a yearning response. 'I knew from the start that it could be like this—and, believe me, sweetheart, this is just the beginning.'

Just the beginning! Saffron felt that her head was swimming, as if she was in the grip of some heated fever that had resulted in burning delirium. If this was only the beginning, then she didn't know how she was going to cope with what was to come—because it *would* come; she knew that without a doubt. It was as inevitable as a summer forest-fire raging through a drought-dry forest—raw, primitively powerful, and totally devastating, shrivelling everything in its path and completely unstoppable. There was no further thought of fight in her mind. One day she would be Niall's—the only question was when and how.

At long last Niall drew away, his sigh reluctant, his hands going to smooth his ruffled hair back into place, to fasten the buttons on his shirt, and even though the gestures seemed to speak of a cool collectedness that indicated an unemotional lack of involvement, Saffron was pleased to see a faint tremor in those strong fingers that revealed the way he wasn't quite as composed as he would like her to believe. As for herself, she was a shattered wreck, limp as a wrung-out cloth, her bones seeming to have melted in the heat of their shared passion, but with the writhing, aching serpent of need deep inside her totally unassuaged and furiously demanding more.

'Look what an effect you have on me!' Niall's laugh was wry and self-deprecating. 'Not only do my workmates think I've gone out of my mind, but I'm as hot as any adolescent on his first date. I said I was too old for making out in cars, but, believe me——' his eyes darkened and his voice became a deep, husky growl '—you'd tempt any man.'

Looking deep into her face once more, he abandoned all pretence at restoring order to his appearance, and bent towards her. But this time his lips had barely brushed hers before, with a groan, he jerked himself upright again.

'Oh, God! This isn't the time or the place. Saffron——'

But Niall's talk of time had drawn Saffron's eyes once more to the clock, an exclamation of shock escaping her as she registered what it said.

'It certainly isn't! Niall, it's almost two—my appointment!'

'Is it really so important?'

'It's vital! I need that contract or A Movable Feast will go under! Niall, please——'

But he was already moving, ramming the key into the ignition and setting the powerful engine roaring as he fastened his seatbelt.

'The mirror——' he said sharply, swinging out on to the road.

'What?' Saffron frowned her confusion.

'Look at yourself in the mirror.'

As soon as she did so, Saffron saw only too clearly just what he meant. She was in no fit state to meet a prospective client, or anyone else for that matter. Her dark hair was like a bird's nest, her lipstick was smudged, her brown eyes were overbright above burning cheeks, and, worst of all, her blouse gaped widely where his urgent hands had tugged it open, exposing the tops of her breasts, and the delicate flesh was marked with red patches from his fierce kisses, his urgent caresses.

With a shocked exclamation, she set about repairing the damage, fastening buttons with frantic haste, tugging a comb through the tangled ebony waves of her hair. She had barely completed the task when Niall, who had ignored all speed-limits on the journey, drew the car up outside her work premises.

'Will I do?' she asked, still breathless from the speed of the necessary readjustment.

Eyes that were a surprisingly cool grey, showing none of the reaction that had darkened them earlier, skimmed over her in a swift, assessing glance.

'You'll do,' he assured her. 'Even Owen's mama couldn't find fault.'

'Oh, I doubt that.' Saffron laughed. 'I'd never be right for her—I'd swear she thinks I'm after her precious son's inehritance. Niall—I have to go——'

'One minute——'

His hand around her arm was firm, holding her with a grip that was so hard it was bordering on painful, and she felt she would bruise where his strong fingers had fastened on her wrist.

'Owen will have to go.' It was an order, not a statement. 'I don't share my women with anyone.'

If only he knew that Owen was no longer a consideration, and hadn't been ever since Niall himself had exploded into her life. But she wasn't going to tell him that, not now, possibly not ever.

'My *women*', was the phrase he had used, and suddenly all her fears came back in a worrying rush.

What was she doing? She had thought that she wanted commitment, the security of a loving marriage like the one her parents and sisters enjoyed, instead she had become entangled with a man she scarcely knew, a man who spoke no words of love but only desire, a man who had openly declared that when he saw what he wanted he went for it without hesitation.

And he wanted her. The shiver of excitement that shot through her at the thought told her that, for now, that was enough.

'Saffron——' There was a warning note in Niall's voice. He hadn't liked her silence. His hand came under her chin, lifting her face up to his.

'Yes!' Desperate to be gone, Saffron would have agreed to anything. 'Now will you please let me go——?'

'Just one more thing,' Niall said, his voice huskily intent. 'I really have to get back to London—sort things out—for a couple of days, at least. There'll be hell to pay if I don't. You do understand?'

This time she could only nod, using her silence to hide her private disappointment at the way that, having, in his opinion, wooed and won her, he could now turn his attention to more pressing matters.

'But I'll be back.' Niall's eyes darkened suddenly, and he pressed warm, soft lips against her cheek. 'I promise,' he whispered, his breath feathering her ear. 'Just as soon as I can get away—I'll be back.'

His words and the gentleness of that kiss eased the ache of disappointment. The intensity of that whispered promise was all that she could have asked for.

Niall's fingertips touched her cheek where his lips had rested a moment before, and in a gesture of infinite tenderness he tucked a stray lock of dark hair behind her ear.

'Think about me,' he murmured, his eyes holding hers.

'Think about me,' Saffron's thoughts echoed dazedly a few moments later when, standing on the pavement outside her office, she watched the powerful car accelerate down the road and turn the corner out of sight. Think about him! She doubted that she'd be able to think about anything else.

CHAPTER EIGHT

SAFFRON studied her reflection in the mirror and frowned at the look of nervousness in the brown eyes staring back at her, the tension in her face echoed by the apprehension twisting her stomach.

It was ten days since she had last seen Niall; two weeks in total since the day he had exploded into her life and turned it upside-down. Since he had returned to London he had been in contact by phone, and had paid one flying visit en route to somewhere else. He had stayed just long enough to take her out to dinner, and had literally left her on the doorstep on their return to her cottage.

'I shouldn't be here, sweetheart,' he had told her. 'In fact, I should be anywhere but here, but I couldn't let another day go by without seeing you.'

There had been a fire at one of their factories, he had said. Arson was suspected, or, at the very least, negligence, and the reputation of the company was at stake. There were other people he could send, who could deputise for him, but he preferred to handle it himself. He had been sure that she would understand.

She did—of course she did—but all the same she still cursed the way that fate seemed to have conspired against her, to keep Niall working and far away from her just at this point in their relationship. His absence gave her too much time to think, to worry about the effect he had had on her, to consider her own behaviour and wonder over and over just what she was doing.

Kate had been characteristically blunt in her response to the situation in which Saffron found herself.

'So whatever happened to, I'm ready for commitment?' she had demanded. 'Are you trying to tell me that Mr White Tornado Forrester is now offering hearts and flowers, wedding-bells and happy-ever-afters when you've only known him for twenty-four hours? Because, quite frankly, he didn't strike me as that kind of man.'

'No,' Saffron had admitted reluctantly. 'I don't think anything could be further from his mind.'

Or from her own, when she was with him; that was the trouble. With Owen she had been looking for security—a future. With Niall, the present was all that mattered, and she was incapable of looking beyond it.

'I think the problem was that I was suffering from post New Year blues. You know, Christmas at home, all those sisters and their husbands—and the new babies——'

Kate, whose only family consisted of a mother who was currently backpacking around Australia with a man fifteen years her junior, smiled rueful sympathy. 'Everyone asking when you were going to join the happy throng——?'

'I thought there had to be more to life than struggling with a business that's dying on its feet.'

'And you thought that sleeping with Owen would provide that?'

Saffron couldn't help laughing at the sceptical expression on her friend's face. 'My relationship with him was another part of my life that seemed to be going nowhere. I thought it just needed a push—some extra input on my behalf. I didn't realise that that, too, was something that was dying on its feet.'

'Owen didn't take too kindly to being given the push?'

'He was furious—called me every name under the sun.
I'm just grateful I didn't tell him about Niall. I didn't
even say there was someone else.'

It was all too new, too fragile. She still couldn't believe it was happening.

'I don't know how he would have reacted if I had.
But I didn't want him to think I'd just broken up with
him because of Niall.'

She didn't want Niall to think that either. The memory
of that arrogant, 'Owen will have to go,' still rankled,
provoking a sense of defiant rebellion. She hadn't just
been following Niall's orders.

'Owen and I had come to the end of our particular
road—the relationship wasn't giving me what I needed,
no matter how much I put into it. That was really brought
home to me the night he stood me up.'

'The night you were all ready to do your sacrificial
lamb act?'

Saffron nodded slowly, suddenly becoming aware of
just how appropriate Kate's words were.

'I didn't decide to sleep with Owen because I just
couldn't help myself—because it was what I *wanted*—
but because of the restlessness I was feeling.'

That restlessness that had driven her to want to im-
prove their relationship somehow—*anyhow*.

'But it shouldn't be like that. If you are to give yourself
to someone it should be because you can't do anything
else, because you feel that you'd die if you don't.' As
she now felt with Niall. 'I was just kidding myself,' she
added ruefully.

'So, what now? I mean, if that was the end of winter
blues, then what are you suffering from now? Belated
spring fever? Early midsummer madness?'

'I don't know, Kate, and to tell you the truth, I don't really care. When I'm with Niall he makes me feel so very different. He excites me, he——'

'You're in love!'

Kate's laughing comment pulled Saffron up short, forcing her to look at herself and her behaviour with a cool clarity of thought that hadn't been possible since she had first encountered Niall.

Was she in love? No, it wasn't possible, not after such a short time. After all, she had only known Niall— what?—two weeks? And in that time she had spent perhaps twenty-four hours in total in his company. She couldn't know him in that time, let alone feel anything deep for him. No, she wasn't in love, but he had knocked her flying—mentally that was. She hadn't been able to get her feet back on solid ground since.

'Don't be silly, Kate!' Her voice wasn't quite as steady as she might have wished. In order to bring herself firmly down to earth, she went on, 'And now we'd better talk about some rather more practical matters—like how we're going to hold A Movable Feast together, for one.'

'Is it really dying on its feet?' Kate asked in some concern.

'Not far off it—the patient's condition is critical, I should say. Apart from Mr Robinson's contract for the bowls club, and a couple of children's birthday parties, we've nothing on our books. We desperately need some more customers, Kate. If we don't get them, we're going to go out of business——'

The sound of the doorbell interrupted Saffron's memories, bringing her back to the present with a rush, with the realisation that while she had brooded Niall's car had pulled up outside, and now the man himself was on her doorstep.

Her heart suddenly set up a new and disturbingly rapid pattern, bringing a rush of colour to her cheeks and making her breathing uneven as she checked her appearance in the mirror again, smoothing down the cream-coloured sweatshirt that she wore with sand-toned Lycra leggings, and pushing a wandering dark strand of hair back into the thick braid that hung down past her shoulders before hurrying to open the door.

'Hi!' Niall dropped a brief kiss on her forehead before strolling into the house as if he was the one who actually owned it. 'I got here earlier than I expected—traffic on the motorway wasn't half as bad as I'd anticipated. Missed me?'

Had she missed him? Saffron knew that she hadn't realised just how much until he was standing there before her, his height and strength seeming to dwarf the tiny proportions of her minuscule peach-and-green-painted living-room. Like her, he was casually dressed, in the supple leather jacket he had worn when he had taken her out to lunch, with a pale green T-shirt and darker green jeans. Everything about him seemed so much bigger and more forceful, even his colouring more dramatic than she remembered, and her heart suddenly seemed to stop at the thought that this strong, devastatingly attractive man—this wonderful specimen of potently concentrated masculinity—had actually travelled all the way from London just to see *her*.

'Hey!' Niall's quiet voice drew her attention. 'You don't look exactly pleased to see me. Is something wrong?'

'Wrong? No, it's just——' The truth broke from her before she had a chance to consider the wisdom or otherwise of revealing it. 'I wasn't really sure that you'd come.'

'And why wouldn't I? I said I would, didn't I?'

'Yes, but——'

'And I never say anything I don't mean—you would do well to remember that.'

His words were laced with an ominous undercurrent that made Saffron shiver faintly, her mood changing abruptly as she was forced to recall his adamant declaration about being able to walk away from anything. She could be in no doubt that he had meant that too.

She had told Kate that she didn't care about the possible consequences of a relationship with him—but was that strictly true? Was she really capable of handling a situation that offered her nothing more than the here and now?

'I'm sorry——' she began, but then Niall's mouth curled into a slow, enticing smile, driving all thought of what she had been about to say from her mind as he held out his hand.

'Come here,' he said softly, and without being quite aware of having moved she was suddenly in his arms and being held up against the hard strength of his body, his warmth reaching her even through her clothes, his scent all around her, as she was kissed with such ruthless efficiency that within seconds her head was spinning deliriously.

'Now do you believe me?' he demanded, and she could only nod silently, her heart singing with happiness, too full to allow her to speak.

All she had ever wanted was right here, beside her, as he let her know with his kisses, his touch, the husky murmur of need that broke from him, that *she* was what he wanted, and that when he had told her so he had meant every word he said.

When Niall moved, taking her with him to the settee and sinking down on it, she was unable to resist, a puppet obeying his every masterful tug on her strings, and she knew that if he was to loosen his grip then, like that puppet with its strings cut, she would collapse in a limp heap on the floor, unable to support herself.

Her mouth opened under his, the provocative teasing of his tongue adding fuel to the fire of passion that flared inside her as she returned his kiss with deliberate provocation, clinging to the muscular strength of his arms and letting her head loll back against the hard support of his shoulder. She was trembling with desire, every nerve alive with excitement as his hands moved lower, sliding under the soft cream cotton of her sweatshirt, the sensation of the warmth of his hard fingers on her skin making her sigh against his mouth and try to strain even closer. Niall wasn't immune to passion either, and she felt the shudder that ran through his long body before, with a harsh groan, he wrenched his mouth from hers, breaking the kiss, and pushed her slightly away from him.

'Niall!' It was a cry of reproach, her voice uneven, her breathing ragged. Why had he stopped? Didn't he know how much she wanted him? Couldn't he feel it in every inch of her slender frame?

'Hold on, sweetheart,' he said in a tone that was rough and thick. 'Don't you think that before we take things further we ought at least to know a little more about each other than just names and occupations?'

'"Before we take things further!" You're very sure of yourself——' Saffron couldn't hide her reaction to Niall's casual confidence.

'And why not?' he returned easily. 'I'm not stupid—or blind. It isn't a matter of *if*, Saffron; the only question is when—and you know that as well as I do.'

There was no way she could deny the truth of his blunt statement. She knew what Niall wanted from her—wasn't it just what she wanted from him? Surely the aching disappointment she had felt at the abrupt cessation of his lovemaking told her that?

'I just don't want to be taken for granted——'

'Oh, Saffron, I could never do that—you're not the sort of lady anyone could take for granted in any way. But if it seemed that way, I'm sorry.' His smile was cajoling, enticing. 'And to prove it, I have a present for you.'

'A present?' Saffron's mood lifted swiftly.

The sound of Niall's laughter as her expression brightened was like balm to her heart, easing the faintly bruised sensation of a moment before.

'What is it?'

The tissue-wrapped package was slim and soft, and when she tore it open it was to find the most beautiful silk scarf she had ever seen, fine and cobweb-delicate. It was shaded only in bronze and gold tones, without a trace of the gaudy scarlet that held such disturbing implications for her, and she was able to accept it without restraint and with no disturbance to her volatile mental equanimity.

'It's gorgeous!' she almost danced to the mirror to fasten it loosely about her throat. 'Perfect! What do you think?' she asked, spinning round to face him.

His eyes, burning like molten silver, gave her her answer without words, and she knew without any hope of salvation that if he held out his arms to her once more she would go straight into them without thought or hesitation. If he said, Come to bed, her response would be just the same, she realised, and the revelation made her close her eyes in confusion, breaking the spell that held them both.

'Let's go for a walk,' Niall said abruptly, the words sounding strangely stiff and tight, as if he had forced them from a painfully dry throat. 'It's a beautiful day, and I've been stuck in offices or the car almost all the time for the past ten days—I could do with some air.'

'We'll go down by the river, if you like,' she said as lightly as she could, leading the way through the kitchen and out into her pocket handkerchief-sized garden, at the bottom of which ran a pathway down to the riverbank.

'Perfect.'

Niall paused for a moment to draw in a deep breath of the clean, fresh air, warmed by the afternoon sun.

'London is no place to be in the spring.'

'You surprise me——'

Saffron spoke quickly to cover her own spontaneous and very sensual reaction. With the sunlight gleaming on his jet-black hair, his jacket now discarded and slung over one shoulder so that she could see how the soft cotton of his T-shirt clung to the strong lines of his shoulders and chest, emphasising the lean maleness of his shape, it was all she could do not to reach for him and kiss him with fierce and inviting passion.

'I thought you were a city man through and through.'

Niall shook his dark head firmly, causing a lock of black hair to fall forward on to his forehead, and Saffron's fingers itched to touch it, feel its silky softness under their tips as she brushed it gently backwards into the rest of the shining mane.

'Not me; not by choice. When you get to know me better you'll see that that's only one side of me.'

When she got to know him better! The words had a wonderfully hopeful sound inside her head, but then, almost immediately, harsh realism brushed aside her happy delusion, dismissing such thoughts as just idle dreams. Niall was with her now because it suited him to be there. He wanted her—the look in his eyes as she had turned from the mirror had left her in no doubt about that—but only for now. She would be wise not to allow herself to hope for any more.

'London's where my offices are—where the contacts, the influences are—but it's no place to live full-time. I've always had a dream of a home in the country somewhere—like yours.'

'But it would hardly be anything like my tiny place. How did you describe it—a doll's house? It suits me fine, but you'd want something more than a little shoebox of a cottage.'

'It wasn't exactly what I had in mind.' Niall's tone was dry. 'But one of these days I'm going to start a hunt for something that is.'

'So what's stopping you?' Because obviously he couldn't want it *enough*. The man who had declared that when he saw what he wanted he went for it wouldn't let just anything hold him back.

Niall's broad shoulders lifted in an offhand shrug.

'The time has never been quite right—and it always seemed a little greedy when I already have a perfectly adequate home in the city. If I had a family, it would be different.'

'So you haven't ruled out the idea of marriage and children?'

The impulsive question escaped before she had time to consider the wisdom of asking it, and she regretted speaking as Niall turned to her, his eyes steely cold and indifferent, all emotion blanked out.

'One day, maybe,' he said, his tone warning her not to press the matter further, so that she was surprised when he added, 'But that's something of a problem when you're as rich as I am. People tend to see you only in terms of figures on a bank statement, and in my experience women find the idea of a large income more of a turn-on than any physical attraction.'

Saffron turned wide, startled brown eyes on his face, shocked by the dark cynicism in his voice, the way his expression had suddenly become distant and remote.

'You can't really think that someone would only want you because of your money!' Was this what was behind his determination to stay in control, his ability to walk away without a backward look?

'It happens,' he drawled laconicaly. 'I've been there——'

'Has there never been anyone you felt mattered more than that? Someone you——'

'Loved?' Niall supplied when she hesitated. 'Whatever love is. There was someone once—her name was Jayne—but I made the mistake of introducing her to my brother.'

'What happened?'

'She decided to marry him instead of me.'

'Oh, God!' The starkness of the declaration, the flatness of his tone, shocked Saffron. 'I'm sorry—that must have hurt terribly.'

Once more that dismissive lift of his shoulders expressed his indifference to any extreme feeling.

'As a matter of fact, it was how little it bothered me that was worrying. It made me realise that what I'd thought was a great passion was in fact no such thing. Anyway, there's no harm done. It's past—over——'

'No looking back,' Saffron couldn't stop herself from murmuring, her voice low, but Niall caught the soft words.

'Exactly. Besides——' his laugh was careless, disturbing in its indifference '—Jayne makes a great sister-in-law—far better than she would have done a wife.'

The next moment he had turned away from her, his action and the way he stared out across the river—running high because of the recent rain—communicating without words the fact that the topic was now closed and that he would not welcome any attempt to reopen it.

'Is this the same river as the one beside the pub where we had lunch?'

'That's right.' It was safer to follow his lead and not risk any argument. 'It runs all the way from here into York and right through the city.'

'I've never been to York—is it as beautiful as they say?'

'It's wonderful—one of my favourite places! It's such a mixture of the old and new—I think you'd love it. Perhaps——'

She broke off hastily, belatedly seeing the danger in saying that perhaps they could visit the city together. To do that was to assume that they had some degree of a future together, but Niall wasn't the sort of man you could make such assumptions about.

'I'd like to go there some time.' Niall's smile told her that he had watched her face and interpreted only too accurately just what had been going through her mind. 'After all, it looks as if I'll be up in Yorkshire for a while—a couple of months at least—while I sort things out at Richards.'

'A couple of months——'

'It's all I can spare. After all, Richards' Rockets is hardly a major concern.'

'You are going to buy the factory, then?'

She couldn't iron out the jerky note in her voice. How much time could he spare for her? She had told herself that she wouldn't ask for a future, but a couple of months seemed like no time at all.

'Why? Don't you think I should?' He had caught the hesitant note, but attributed it to some totally different explanation.

'I—I'm not sure.'

If she had wanted to make sure that he stayed in Kirkham she would have done better to be more enthusiastic, but somehow she was incapable of speaking anything but the exact truth. She also had the uneasy feeling that, if she didn't, Niall would know.

'I mean—there's nothing wrong with the company, except perhaps that it's a little old-fashioned.'

'I had noticed.'

'Owen's father wasn't well for the last year or more of his life. He rather let things go...'

'And how.' Niall's mouth twisted cynically. 'And his son didn't bother to make much effort either. The whole place needs a bomb putting under it.'

'It's not exactly Owen's cup of tea—his interests lie elsewhere.'

'In a night-club called the Safari, to be precise.'

'You know?'

'He has mentioned it.' Niall stopped abruptly, spinning her round to face him. 'Come on, Saffron, what exactly are you trying to say?'

In the sunlight, his grey eyes gleamed like the blade of a well-sharpened knife, and Saffron suddenly felt uncomfortably like some small, vulnerable insect impaled on its point.

'It's just—I wonder if your money might not be better spent elsewhere. I mean—— Owen——'

'Owen's trying to bump up the price to well over the odds—asking for far more than the place is worth in order to get his share of the night-club and still make a profit? Is that it?'

'I—yes.'

Saffron felt vaguely foolish. Of course he'd known all along; he wouldn't be in the position he was now, with a reputation for being something of a genius in the business world, without the sort of clear-minded acumen that could match Owen a thousand times over.

'I just wanted you to know——'

'Which I appreciate, but what concerns me more is your personal relationship with Mr Richards.'

If those light eyes had been bright before, now they were practically translucent.

'Are you checking up on me—making sure that I obeyed orders?' she parried with a sudden flare of defiance.

'Do I need to?' he returned, his tone implying little doubt that she would have done exactly as he said. 'And it wasn't an order. I suggested——'

'Oh, it was a suggestion, was it? I'm sorry—I don't know you well enough to tell the difference.'

'My secretary could enlighten you.' Niall was completely unabashed. 'So, what have you done about Richards?'

For a second she was sorely tempted to tell him that she had done nothing at all, but then she rethought hastily. After all, he would find out for himself soon enough.

'I don't have a personal relationship with Owen any more—but that's not because of you.' She wouldn't give him the satisfaction of thinking that he commanded and she jumped. 'I realised that we weren't going anywhere—and I wanted more out of life than that. I didn't say anything about us,' she added, not sure how he would take that.

But Niall simply nodded. 'We'll leave it that way, then. There's no need for anyone to know our business. Small towns can become a hotbed of gossip.'

'I learned that fast enough when I moved here.' Saffron laughed. 'My efforts to set up A Movable Feast were the subject of an interest that's only just beginning to settle down. They'll be talking enough anyway if you take over Richards,' she added wryly. 'They're reluctant to accept anyone new around here. You'll have to work hard on public relations—coming from London, particularly.'

'You seem to have managed to.'

'Oh, well, I'm hardly from the *South*. Lincolnshire is at least north of Watford—and I did have Kate and Owen to help me settle in. It helped having the backing of the son of the area's major employer.'

'So why did you move away from home in the first place?'

'Why does anyone? Independence—proving yourself—and I wanted to assert my individuality. I suppose I felt that more than most, being the baby of such a large family.'

'All those sisters,' Niall murmured smilingly.

'I like being part of a big family! I know it's not exactly fashionable nowadays, but——'

'Hey!' Niall caught hold of the hand with which she was gesticulating furiously. 'Don't be so damn prickly! You really are defensive about your family, aren't you? Did I say anything critical?'

'No...' Saffron admitted. 'But people usually do. I'm sorry—I just thought——'

'You mean, you didn't think,' he reproved. 'Do you usually overreact like this?'

'You don't know the half of it! All my life I've been teased about my family. When I was at school there were so many whispered comments, or laughter behind my back——'

'I'm not laughing. So, tell me. What other skeletons do you have lurking in your cupboards? You have five sisters—and, personally, I think that if they're all as lovely as you, then there couldn't be too many of them. What else?'

'My father...' Saffron murmured, the edgy, defensive feeling partly soothed by his casual compliment. But, even so, the words wouldn't come.

'Richards said something about him being an intellectual—absorbed in his books. Ruane? The only man I know by that name is the one who writes on the derivation of placenames.'

The sharp grey eyes caught Saffron's uneasy movement.

'Is he some relation to Turner Ruane?'

'Not some relation.' Saffron was surprised that Niall had heard of her father, let alone was aware of his obscure field of work. 'He *is* Turner Ruane.'

'But he must be——'

'Positively ancient,' Saffron cut in sharply. 'Old enough to be anyone else's grandfather—or even great-grandfather. I've heard them all before. And, yes, he was nearly fifty when I was born—Mum was forty-three——'

She broke off in consternation as Niall threw back his head and laughed.

'Is that all? Saffron, you had me worried that there was some terrible dark secret in your family.'

'My schoolfriends thought there was.' Saffron wasn't used to this sort of response. 'They couldn't get their heads round the fact that my parents were still—had still been——'

'Making love?' Niall supplied, when embarrassment overcame her. 'At that incredibly advanced age!'

The mockery in his voice was aimed at those so-called friends, she realised, not at her or her family.

'Why do adolescents think that they're the only ones who know about sex? I would have been proud to think that my parents still cared about each other—and you must have been very much a wanted child.'

'That's not how Agnes Richards sees it. She was frankly aghast. She sees my father as some weird, other-worldly nutty professor, shut away in his ivory tower, with no sense of reality, making no practical contribution to things.'

'And a factory that produces fireworks is *practical*?' The mockery was sharper now.

'Oh, well, that was an embarrassment to her—she only tolerated it when it was keeping her in the manner to which she'd grown accustomed. That was why she wasn't keen on my part in Owen's life. I think she thought he'd use their money to support my business—one that was rapidly failing around me.'

'Is that a fact, or just what Ma Richards would think?'

There was an odd note in Niall's voice, and the arm he had slung around her shoulders felt tense suddenly.

'Both,' Saffron admitted. 'I'm afraid that the market for freelance caterers isn't exactly huge. What I need is a very wealthy benefactor—someone to bail me out and put the whole thing on a sound footing.'

'Me?'

Niall had come to a halt again and was staring out at the river once more. After a moment he took his arm from her shoulders and bent down to pick up a large, flat pebble, aiming carefully before sending it skimming across the smooth, gleaming surface.

'Would you like me as your benefactor?'

If only! Saffron couldn't help thinking. It would solve her financial problems at a stroke. But then reality intervened, with the recollection of his cynical comment about the emotional consequences of being a rich man. His question had seemed almost *too* casual.

'Are you trying to buy up the whole of Kirkham?'

It didn't sound quite as it had inside her head; the teasing note she had aimed for came out with a flirtatious inflexion that made it seem as if she was trying to probe deeper rather than refute his suggestion.

'Would you think it would be worth my while?' To her relief, he matched her teasing. 'Would I get a good return on my investment?'

He had turned to face her again, eyes narrowed against the sun, and her heart lurched sharply on a wave of intense physical awareness.

'Oh, I don't see why not!' It was suddenly an effort to speak, with her heart beating high up in her throat so that she felt breathless and light-headed. 'Play your cards right and you could have anything you wanted.'

'Could I?'

Everything had changed. The lightness of his voice was suddenly not echoed by the flare of sensuality in his eyes, the incandescent blaze of primitive desire that was somehow shocking in contrast to his carefully civilised tone.

The second stone he had picked up to throw after the first fell from his loosened grip, to land unheeded on the grass as his other hand reached out to draw her close, the strength of his arm coming round her, holding her like a steel band, as hard fingers under her chin tilted her face up towards his.

'Could I really, Saffron? Could I have *anything* at all?'

The last words were murmured against her mouth, his lips barely brushing hers, but it was as if the delicate touch was a blazing brand, scorching right to her deepest soul, marking her out as his and drawing from her a moan of response and yearning as fiery need raged through every cell in her body.

'Anything!' she choked, pressing swift, feverish kisses on the lean planes of his cheeks, feeling the roughness of the day's growth of beard against her sensitive skin, inhaling the scent of his body. 'You know you don't have to ask!'

The thought of a future, of more time with Niall, no longer concerned her. All that mattered was here and now. And here was in Niall's arms, held so close that she could feel the rapid, uneven beat of his heart, could tangle her fingers in the sunwarmed silk of his hair. Now was being kissed until her senses reeled, until her bones became as soft and pliant as warm wax and she melted against him, waiting only to be moulded as he wanted, so that she made no protest when his hands slid under the soft cotton of her top, drifting upwards with agonisingly delicate deliberateness to the taut sensitivity of her breasts.

'I think we know all we need to know about each other,' Niall muttered, his voice thick and rough. 'This is enough——'

He kissed her again, making a deep sound of pleasure low in his throat as she let her hands wander over the tight muscles of his back and shoulders, slipping her fingers in at the neck to feel the satin warmth of his skin. But then abruptly his mood changed.

'Oh, God!' Niall's raw-toned exclamation slashed through the sensual haze that enclosed her, dragging her back to a painful awareness of reality. 'No—not here— not the first time. Saffron—honey——'

He stopped her when she would have kissed him once more, his breathing ragged and uneven.

'Saffron!' Niall's laughter was low and sensual, with a slightly shaken edge to it. 'Are you really such a wild and wanton creature that you'd let me take you here and now, on the grass, where anyone could see? But, of course, I should have expected it...'

At last, cold reality penetrated the burning haze of Saffron's thoughts. She knew what was in his mind. He was thinking of their first meeting, of the scarlet basque and tiny lacy suspender belt—those flirtatious, provocative garments that had given him quite the wrong impression of her.

Or had they? Because the trouble was that she knew that if he hadn't stopped when he had, if he had pushed a little more, pressed her just the tiniest bit harder, if he *had* wanted to make love to her right here and now, on the soft grass of the riverbank, then she would not have been able to stop him.

'Come on——'

Niall slid an arm around her waist and pulled her so close that the muscular length of his leg was against her slender limb from hip to knee, his hand resting with warm intimacy under the curve of her breast. The immediate and electric rush of warmth through her body once again told her a disturbing truth. The problem with the way she felt about this man was not whether she could become the sensual woman he believed her to be, but whether, having once given the passion he woke in her free rein, she could ever find a way to get it back under control again.

CHAPTER NINE

MUCH later, Saffron found herself wondering how she had ever got home. At times the short journey had seemed to drag on forever, each step covering only the tiniest space, at others it had been as if they were part of a film that was being played at the wrong speed, every action jerky and unnatural, the countryside flashing past at an alarming rate. Sometimes it had seemed that her legs would not support her, and that only the strength of Niall's arm was keeping her upright, moving her inexorably in the direction he wanted her to go.

And then, at last—or did she mean too soon?—they were at the gate to the cottage garden, and she didn't know whether she was on her head or her heels emotionally.

'We're here,' she managed inanely.

'Yes,' Niall said, 'we're here.'

His tone made his words much more than a statement of fact, and suddenly all her confidence deserted her, replaced by a churning sense of panic deep in her stomach, so that she practically raced up the path and into the kitchen.

'I'll make some coffee.' She spoke rapidly to cover her nervousness. 'I'm sure you could do with a drink.'

'No.'

The single, flat syllable came starkly, completely destroying what little remained of her composure, and she couldn't help but be aware of the way that Niall's silvery eyes watched her pointless, jittery movements around the room, as a collector might watch a rare butterfly he had trapped in a jam jar, beating its wings against the sides.

'Well, then, something to eat. Let me make you some——'

'I'm not hungry,' Niall cut in harshly.

When she stopped dead in the middle of the room, her wide, soft brown eyes going to his face, seeing the determination, the raw need stamped on its strong-boned features, he took a single step towards her, reaching out one strong hand and catching hold of her own nerveless fingers, drawing her gently but inexorably towards him.

'At least, not for food,' he murmured, and his eyes were no longer silver-light, but dark and smoky, his voice husky with a desire that she knew could not be communicated in words, but which coiled around her taut body, warming and loosening the tightly-strung nerves, melting her resistance, sending electrically charged impulses through pleasure spots she hadn't known existed.

'Do you want to eat?' Niall asked, and she shook her head slowly.

'No...'

And with that single syllable it was decided. There was no going back. But Saffron knew that was now the furthest thing from her mind. The only way she could think of was forward, forward into the unknown of this relationship. She closed her eyes and took a deep breath as Niall's lips came down on hers, sealing their unspoken agreement with a kiss that seared right to her heart, branding her as his, now and for whatever future they might share.

It started gently, the touch of his mouth light and surprisingly delicate, but in the space of a heartbeat it was as if that brief contact had fuelled a blazing, roaring conflagration. 'Light the blue touchpaper and stand well back,' Niall had said, describing the sparks that flew between them, but in the moment that their lips met Saffron knew that the fuse that had been lit at their first meeting had now burned away completely. The resulting explosion, inside her head and in every cell of her body, made her feel as if her blood had turned to liquid fire, melting her bones, so that she sagged against Niall and would have fallen if his arms hadn't come round her, sweeping her off her feet and carrying her out of the kitchen and towards the stairs.

In her room, he lowered her gently on to the bed, his hands coming up to cup her face as he looked deep into her eyes.

'You won't regret this,' he told her softly. 'I promise—— '

'No—— ' Hastily Saffron placed a finger against his mouth, silencing him. 'No promises.'

She didn't need him to say anything to convince her that this was right; couldn't bear him to make any promises he couldn't keep. All that mattered was here and now, in this room, in her arms...

'Kiss me—— '

Reaching up, she drew him down to her, her lips replacing her finger, communicating the gnawing, aching need that could never be assuaged by words, and with a sound that was half a sigh, half a groan deep in his throat, he came down on to the bed beside her, pulling her close to him with an urgency that spoke of the struggle he had had to keep his feelings under control.

Saffron welcomed that urgency with a tiny cry of delight. The time for hesitation, for restraint, for thought was past; now she wanted only to feel, to be taken out of herself and into a world where nothing existed beyond their two bodies and the glorious, mind-blowing sensations they could create between them.

'Is this what you want?' Niall whispered as he eased her sweatshirt from her, swiftly unclasping the front fastening of her bra and lowering his head to press his hot mouth against her breasts. 'And this——?'

She could only respond with a choked, incoherent sound of pleasure, lifting shaking hands to tangle in the jet darkness of his hair. She was incapable of words, only knew that she had never known sensation like this, a pleasure so sharp it was like a shaft of pain. She had never known what it felt like to be so desired, so wonderfully wanton, so supremely, totally female.

Her thoughts shattered, her fingers clenching in the black, silky strands, as Niall's mouth found one nipple and closed over it, tugging softly. It seemed as if the serpent of need that she had felt was now wide awake and desperately hungry, stretching its gleaming body and swaying restlessly, driven by purely primitive desire.

'Oh, Niall—Niall!'

His name was a restless, desperate litany on her lips, her voice coming and going unevenly as Niall's lips scorched a burning trail from one breast to the other, subjecting the second one to the same savage pleasure and reducing her to a mindless, shuddering state of blind delight.

'You're beautiful,' he muttered thickly against her sensitised skin, the warm, featherlight caress of his words making her arch her back in uninhibited response. 'I've wanted this since the moment I first saw you in that ridiculously provocative outfit——'

It was exactly what she hadn't wanted him to say. She didn't want him to think of that woman, the woman who wasn't really her.

'Niall...' Her voice was just a whisper, so that he had to bring his dark head down close to her lips to catch it. 'I—I'm not very good at this——'

His laughter was low and soft, his mouth curving warmly.

'Oh, Saffron, sweetheart, you don't have to worry—this isn't some sort of test. It will be fine—trust me. Just relax——'

And she did trust him—completely. In that moment she would have given him her soul if he had asked for it. Because it seemed that Niall, with his burning kisses, his fiendishly knowledgeable touch, that seemed to know exactly where to caress her in order to appease one hunger and awaken another in the same shattering moment, was the man she had been created for. This was so right, it had to have been written into the script of her life from the moment she had been born. It was as inevitable and necessary to life itself as every breath she drew into her body.

Impatient now, fingers clumsy with need, they found buttons, fastenings, until their clothes fell discarded to the floor. The silence of the early evening was broken by Saffron's small sharp cries of pleasure as Niall's kisses and caresses woke responses that were even stronger and more demanding than before.

'Yes—oh, yes——'

The word beat at her brain like the wild, uneven pulsing of her heart, and under her cheek she heard it echoed in the ragged breathing that told of Niall's loosening grip on his control as those tormenting hands moved lower, touching the very core of her, so that he knew without a word having to be spoken that she was open to him, the crescendo of passion reaching its peak as the hard, muscular length of his body moved over hers.

Helplessly she clung to him, her fingers digging into the silken warmth of his skin, into the powerful strength beneath it. Niall's groan of pleasure as their bodies became one mingled with her own cry of shocked delight before the sound was crushed back into her throat by the pressure of his lips on hers.

'I knew it could be like this,' he muttered against her lips. 'Now you see why I had to act, why I had to separate you from Richards. Would he ever be able to do this to you?'

Hot fingers scorched a trail over the sensitised tip of one aching breast and Saffron cried aloud at the exquisite pleasure he was inflicting on her.

'Could he make you respond like this? Could he make you beg for his kisses—his touch?'

'No——' It was a moan of torment and delight that escaped her. 'No—never—never——'

'Of course not. He never knew you—but I did. I knew you could be like this—that together——'

He broke off on a sharp gasp as beneath him she moved with intuitive eroticism, needing to feel him deeper within her as she reached for the culmination that she knew was now so close—so close...

But when it came she was totally unprepared for the intensity of it, for the explosions that went off inside her, the rockets that soared upwards in a stream of multicoloured sparks in her mind. From somewhere she heard a voice, gasping Niall's name, almost sobbing in reaction, and was shocked to realise that it was her own, and that as the white-hot blaze of ecstasy slowly subsided to the shuddering, sweat-slicked exhaustion of repletion, she had no idea what she had said, having lost all control of her tongue as well as her body.

But Niall seemed to need no words as his breathing gradually slowed to a comfortable pace and he curled strong arms around her, drawing her into the warmth of his body and holding her there, safe and secure and totally at peace, until relaxation drifted into deep and totally restful sleep, with her head pillowed on his chest, her dark hair spread out across his shoulder.

She had no idea how long they lay like that, legs tangled together, his arms still holding her. She only knew that at some point she was wakened by the warm, enticing touch of his wandering hands, the soft caress of his fingers arousing that yearning need in her slowly and surely, until she was once more reaching for him, clinging to him, wanting to feel the deep, fulfilment of his love-making all over again.

When she finally surfaced fully enough to become aware of her surroundings, it was to find that night had closed in on them while they lay oblivious to its approach, and that now her small bedroom was in darkness, only the weak rays of the half-moon coming in through the uncurtained window giving enough light by which to see. As Saffron stirred tentatively Niall's arm tightened about her waist, and he lifted his head slightly to whisper in her ear.

'Now I *am* hungry. Starving, in fact. What about you?'

As if in answer to his question, her stomach growled a protest at being left empty for so long, and she felt rather than saw the smile that curled his wide mouth, the laughter that shook his strong body.

'Enough said. Do you have any food in this doll's house of yours?'

'Plenty. Enough even to feed an outsize brute like you several square meals.' Indignation coloured her tone, causing Niall to lever himself up, supported on one elbow, and look down into her moonlit face.

'It seems I've put my foot in it somewhere, without meaning to. So, tell me, sweetheart, why so huffy?'

That soft-toned 'sweetheart' almost defeated her, all the more so because it was accompanied by a lazy, sleepy smile, those silver eyes gleaming warmly under heavy lids.

'I wish you wouldn't refer to my home so disparagingly! I realise that it must seem microscopic to you when compared to what you're used to, but I love it! It may only be two up, two down, but it's all mine—and after years of no privacy, of sharing with one or more sisters, that means a lot, I can tell you.'

'All right, I'm sorry!'

The defensive gesture Niall made with his hands, lifting them up before his face as if to protect himself from her furious glare, was belied by the laughter in his eyes.

'I won't speak ill of the place ever again—it's a little palace! It wasn't meant to sound disparaging,' he went on, sobering abruptly. 'And I certainly never intended to compare it to my place in London——'

'No, I don't suppose you did.'

Saffron didn't want him to talk about his home or London. To do so seemed too much like a bitter reminder that he had a life that was completely separate from this time spent with her, a life to which he would eventually return, leaving her behind.

'Now—what about a meal?' Hastily she turned the conversation on to less worrying topics. 'What would you like to eat?'

'Don't go to any trouble.'

Niall stretched lazily, rolling over on to his back and freeing her from the sensual imprisonment of the warm weight of his body.

'Just something light——' a grin surfaced, wickedly teasing, like the glinting glance he slanted in her direction '—so that I can get my strength back...'

'Right——' Saffron flung back the covers and swung her legs out of bed. 'Would you like a shower?'

'If you'll share it with me.'

The grin had widened, becoming positively lascivious, and belatedly Saffron became aware of her naked state, her embarrassment made all the worse by the fact that the bronze and gold scarf which she had tied round her throat still remained at her neck, like some long-ago slave necklace.

'I don't think that's a good idea.' Hastily she reached for her robe and pulled it on. 'It's late already, and if I don't get on it will be midnight before we eat.'

It was foolish to feel so awkward, now, after all the intimacies they had shared, but the truth was that she had no experience of anything like this, and the sight of Niall, so dark and strong, so devastatingly *male*, in the intimacy of her white and gold bedroom, where no man had ever set foot before, had put her completely off-balance.

'OK.' Niall's agreement came with surprising equanimity when she had nerved herself for something more. 'You're probably right,' he added with a swift glance at the clock. 'But I will take that shower, if you don't mind——'

'Be my guest.'

Saffron's heart was starting to race uncomfortably. Niall's movement, small as it was, had made the covers drop from the muscled lines of his chest down to his narrow waist. If he sat up any more, then the whole of his magnificent body would be revealed... With an effort she dragged her eyes away, turning to the door.

'There are fresh towels in the airing cupboard——'

Get a grip! she told herself as she hurried downstairs. Niall was a sophisticated man of the world. He must have been in this situation many times—it was nothing new to him! He would treat it simply as a natural development—and would expect her to do the same. She had no chance of convincing him that she could handle the sort of casual affair he clearly wanted if she didn't show a little more sophistication herself.

She had set the kitchen table, prepared a salad, put tiny new potatoes on to boil and was busy beating eggs for a substantial omelette by the time she heard Niall's footsteps descending the stairs.

'Won't be a minute,' she said, putting her head round the door, and immediately wishing she hadn't as the sight of Niall, fresh from his shower, with his jet-black hair still damp and showing a disconcerting tendency to curl at his temples and the nape of his neck, was thoroughly disturbing to her carefully imposed mental equilibrium. 'Would you like a drink?'

'No thanks.'

He was looking around him with interest, taking in the details of her living-room.

'Do you realise that this is the first time I've really seen your home properly? The other times I've been in this room we haven't exactly stayed around for long.'

His smile was one of sensual satisfaction, like the expression of a well-fed tiger, so that she knew he was recalling just why they hadn't lingered.

'I like your home, Saffron. It may only be small but it has character.' His gesture indicated the embroidered shawl draped over the settee, the toning pastel cushions.

'It didn't look at all like this when I moved in—it was a real dump then. I did all the painting myself, and made the curtains,' she added with a touch of pride. 'Mum and a couple of my sisters wanted to come and help, or at least do some of the sewing, but I wanted it to be all my own. They would have hated my choice of colours— or tried to pass on things from their homes that they thought I could use. Sometimes being the baby of the family can be a real pain.'

'They won't let you grow up?'

'That's about it—that's why I could never have stayed in Lincolnshire. There were too many Ruanes—too much family. I had to find myself—develop my own individuality.'

Niall glanced round the room again. 'It looks like you've managed to do that.'

'Mmm.' Saffron's smile was full of satisfaction. 'I've just about got it how I want—— What's wrong?' she asked, seeing the way his head had suddenly turned and he seemed to be listening hard.

'Is there something cooking that could——?' He didn't have to finish the sentence.

'The potatoes!'

Niall followed as she dashed back into the kitchen and turned down the heat under the pan, leaning one hip up against the worktop and watching her as she wiped up the spilled water and then poured the egg mixture into a pan. A glossy magazine lay on the windowsill and he picked it up, studying it for a moment.

'Do you have a subscription to every magazine under the sun? Or have you raided a newsagent's lately? The magazines——' he added when she turned a puzzled frown on him '—you must have half a dozen on the coffee-table in there—and——'

'Oh, that's a weakness of mine.' Saffron concentrated fiercely on her cooking. 'Another result of being one of six.'

'How?' Niall questioned curiously. 'I don't quite follow the logic.'

'Well, bedrooms weren't the only things we had to share. There wasn't a lot of money to go around so treats like magazines were fairly strictly rationed. We did get them, but never one each. So there was a strict rota— one week Mollie got it first, then Karis, and so on. It was great when you were number one or two, but when you had to wait until *everyone* had read it—that could take all week. Some of my sisters were very slow readers! So now, my idea of a treat is a brand-new, pristine, glossy magazine—untouched by human hand.'

She slipped the finished omelettes on to warmed plates and put them on the table.

'Supper's ready——'

She broke off in surprise and shock as Niall moved, but not to sit down. Instead, he slid a hand under her chin, lifting her face to his, and placed a swift, firm kiss on her half-open mouth.

'Wh-what was that for?'

'Just wanted to.' Niall laughed at her stunned expression. 'This looks good,' he went on, settling himself in a chair and reaching for the bowl of salad. 'And I suppose that you'll justify all those clothes upstairs in much the same way as the magazines?'

'Well, if you'd spent as much of your life in hand-me-downs as I have——'

Saffron stopped dead at the realisation of what his remark meant, the pan falling from her hand and landing in the sink with a clatter.

'You've been poking round my bedroom?'

'Oh, come on Saffron.' His tone mocked her indignation. 'I'd have to be completely blind to miss the fact that your one small wardrobe is bursting at the seams. I didn't have to look inside.'

'I'd still prefer it if you respected my privacy.'

'My, I have ruffled your feathers, haven't I? Don't worry, sweetheart, I'm not like your family—I'm not about to take over and dictate how you run your life or decorate your precious nest. What's really bugging you, Saffron?' he went on, when she continued to glare at him. 'It can't just be that you're worried about what I might think of your clothes. After all, I'm already well aware of the fact that what you were wearing on our first meeting isn't exactly typical of your usual style.'

'But you would say it was more revealing of my character.'

'Well, let's say that it was an interesting pointer to a side of you that perhaps isn't quite so obvious to everyone.'

'And that's the side——'

'Damn it, no it isn't!' Niall broke in on her angrily, anticipating what she had been about to say. 'I am not so shallow as to make up my mind about you—or anyone—on the strength of a first impression.'

Reaching out, he caught hold of her hand and drew her gently towards him, his strength making a nonsense of her stubborn determination to resist.

'And I'm well aware of the fact that there's more to you than met the eye at our first meeting.'

Deliberately he let his silver gaze slide to the point at the neck of her robe where her breasts curved under the towelling, and when he lifted his eyes to her face again his smile was hard to resist.

'So, is it so terrible that I want to know as much as I can about you?'

Put like that, she could hardly say yes, could she?

'No, of course not.' She managed to smile, sitting down opposite him. 'And I admit to loving new clothes. Though, of course, I'll have to stop buying them now——'

'Why's that?'

'Can't afford them. Most of what's in my wardrobe was bought during the first heady months, when A Movable Feast was actually making a profit. And, of course, some were presents——'

'From Owen?' Niall put in, when a reluctance to bring the other man's name into the conversation made her hesitate.

Saffron nodded. 'I realise that really they were bought more for his sake than mine—Owen liked to project the right sort of image—we were always out somewhere. So of course I had to look the part.'

'I always knew the man was a fool,' Niall growled.

'But I think it's your turn now.' Saffron wanted to get well away from the subject of Owen. 'You know about my family—it's time you told me about yours.'

'Nothing so interesting or numerous as your crowd,' Niall said, helping himself to potatoes. 'I only have one brother.'

'The one who married the girl—I'm sorry.' Saffron cursed herself for her foolishness in touching on the prickly subject again.

'No problem. I told you, it's over—she chose the right brother.'

'Is he older or younger than you?' she asked, simply for something to say.

'Older—but only by eighteen months. My parents fully intended to stop at one, but nature thought otherwise, and I was what Mother calls her happy accident. Andrew looks a lot like me but we're very different characters—chalk and cheese. Andy's a university lecturer—in philosophy—and he's happily settled into marriage with a two-year-old daughter and twins on the way.'

'Twins!' Saffron choked on a mouthful of omelette. 'Do twins run in your family?'

'My father has a twin sister—but you needn't worry.' The grey eyes looked deep into her stunned brown ones. 'I'll always make sure you're protected—as I did tonight. There'll be no risk.'

He had seen her consternation, the tangle of emotions in her face, and had misinterpreted her reaction. Saffron knew that she ought to feel thankful that he had no inkling of the real reason for her distress. He must never know that she had suddenly been prey to a weak and foolish longing to know what Niall's children would look like—twin boys or girls, with his black hair and clear, light-coloured eyes...

'Are you sure you won't have a drink?' It was an effort to speak naturally. 'There's wine——'

'Not when I'm driving, thanks.'

'Oh, but—driving?' The full impact of what he had said hit home. 'Where——'

'I have to get back to the hotel. My secretary has probably left all sorts of messages for me. I only took the time to let her know where I was staying before I came on here.'

But he had done that. Saffron's appetite suddenly deserted her.

'I'm surprised you didn't phone Owen while you were at it—perhaps arrange a few meetings...'

Her voice was tart, disguising the hurt she felt. For a brief space of time she had let herself live in a delusion, allowed herself to think he put her first in his life, and it was only now, when it had been stripped away from her, that she saw just how much that dream had meant to her.

'I am here to work, Saffron. Officially, this trip is business, not pleasure.'

'And me? What heading do I come under?'

Niall's lips curved into a smile that warmed the rather cool expression that had made his face distant a moment before.

'You know you could never be anything other than pleasure.' The smile grew, becoming sensual in a way that matched the gleam that turned those silver eyes translucent. 'So much so that my hotel bed is going to feel hellishly empty without you.'

'I could always come with you,' Saffron suggested, her sense of hurt slightly appeased by his huskily seductive words.

But Niall shook his head with a decisiveness that left no room for further argument.

'I never mix business and pleasure—it's a combination that just doesn't work. Besides, I thought we agreed to keep things private. If you turned up at my hotel the whole town would soon be talking. Now, where did I leave my jacket?'

'In my room——'

It was at the foot of her bed, discarded in the heat of their passion—a passion that seemed to have cooled so very rapidly, on Niall's part at least. But then, almost every action, every word he said, drove home to her the fact that his feelings were nothing like her own. With a struggle she schooled her features into a detachment to match Niall's as he came back down the stairs, the leather jacket slung over one shoulder.

'I'll be in touch.'

She couldn't believe the lightness of his tone. Was this the same man who had held her so close, whose voice, raw and rough with desire, had whispered such erotic compliments in her burning ears only an hour or so before? If he had ever felt that blazing desire, now it was well damped-down and totally under control.

'You know where I am.' Her smile switched on and off like a neon sign, and she fumbled with the handle as she opened the door.

'Hey—don't look like that. I'll only be a few miles down the road. We have a couple of very exciting months ahead of us.'

A couple of months—and then what? Did she have to ask? He'd made it only too plain from the start.

'Come here——'

Reaching out, Niall caught hold of the bronze scarf that she had forgotten was still round her throat. Pulling gently on it, he drew her near enough to kiss her thoroughly, then let her go, running one strong hand through the tumbled dark hair that fell in wild abandon on to her shoulders.

'Sleep well, sweetheart . . .' And with a careless wave he was gone.

'Sleep well'! 'Only a few miles down the road'! Saffron felt that never before had she understood the meaning of so near and yet so far. Niall was here in Kirkham, with her and yet not truly *with* her. She was just a passing fancy to him, another of those things that he wanted and so was determined to have—and, like a fool, she was weak enough to accept that little from him.

Slowly, with an empty ache deep inside her, Saffron locked up and headed upstairs, unable to face the washing-up until morning. The sight of her untidy bed, the tangled sheets and covers evidence of the passionate activity that had filled the early hours of the evening, made her push her hand into her mouth, biting down hard on her fingers against the cry of pain that almost escaped her. She had told herself that she could cope with the sort of affair Niall wanted, but now she was prey to terrible doubts on that score. Could she really go through with this? And yet, as she felt the soft cotton of her towelling robe brush against skin still sensitised by the urgent touch of Niall's hands, nipples still faintly raw from his kisses, she knew there was no way she could deny herself the excitement, the fulfilment she had felt in his arms.

She tidied up the damp towels Niall had used, steeling her senses against the sensual impact of the scent of his body that still lingered on them, and moved to open the wash-basket, meaning only to drop them in and close the lid. But the sight of the scarlet strips of silk, the basque, suspender belt and lacy panties that still lay at the bottom of the container, thrown there in haste two weeks before and never touched since then, stopped her dead.

She had known something was missing from her life, and had decided, quite rationally, that passion—or at least sex—was the vital element things lacked. And so she had bought those ridiculous garments—seductive underwear as unsubtle as a stripper's provocative outfit— and decked herself out in them in order to play a part, and the truth was that a part was all it had been.

'The sacrifical lamb,' Kate had called her, and looking back at herself, sitting in this house, decked out in all her tawdry glory, waiting for Owen, Saffron was appalled at how accurate the description was. She had been prepared to give herself to Owen in a sense of sacrifice, to fill an emptiness that she had thought meant she needed more from him, when in fact it should have told her quite the opposite. She had tried to force herself to feel something she could never feel, and she could only be thankful that she had never actually gone through with it. How much more empty she would have felt then.

With Niall, it had been so very different. With him, she hadn't needed any of those 'props', any fancy dress, and when the time had come there had been no hesitation, no doubts, and even now, whatever the future held, she had no regrets.

So what made the difference? Standing there, clutching the damp towels to her like some sort of talisman, she found that her heart actually seemed to stop for a

moment as she faced a truth that was at once so simple
and yet so desperately, hopelessly complicated that it
would affect the rest of her life, for better or worse.

She had had no doubts, no fears with Niall because
he was the man she loved—the man to whom she had
given her heart and soul in the same moment that she
had given him her body.

CHAPTER TEN

'NOT another bookshop!'

Saffron's voice was full of a resigned exasperation that had Niall pausing in mid-stride, his foot on the step up to the shop doorway.

'We must have been into every one in the city.'

'Just this one. I want to look for——'

'Oh, go on!'

Saffron laughed her defeat. It would take a far harder heart than she possessed to refuse him anything when he turned on that boyishly appealing charm, that devastating smile, even though she knew only too well that it was deliberately calculated to have just that affect.

'But don't expect me to stand around and wait while you become lost in some musty old tome.'

'There won't be any musty tomes in here!' Niall protested. 'We've exhausted all the secondhand shops.'

'Exhausted is the word. And they were definitely dusty, if not musty—as I know to my cost,' Saffron grumbled, rueful eyes going to the dark streak which marred her ivory cotton sleeveless tunic and skirt. Niall, however, had managed to keep his cool linen suit and black T-shirt immaculate as always. 'My feet are aching and I'm dying of thirst.'

'Then the next stop will be somewhere for tea—I promise.'

'Betty's?' Saffron asked cajolingly, her spirits lifting. 'You really can't come to York and not have tea at Betty's. I tell you what,' she added at Niall's nod of agreement, 'we'll probably have to queue for a table—it's always packed, even this late on in the summer—so why don't I go on ahead and you can meet me there? Davygate, remember? Bottom of this street and turn left.'

The queue inside the famous tearooms was every bit as long as she had anticipated, spilling out on to the pavement, but, knowing how efficiently the staff dealt with things, clearing tables and seating people as soon as possible, she was content to wait outside, enjoying the warmth of the late August sun.

As she leaned back against the wall, she let her mind drift back over the past three months—months that had brought her some of the best moments of her life. Being able to spend time with Niall, to see him, talk to him, to make love with him and, above all else, to love him, had filled her days with a joy and brightness, a sense of purpose such as she had never known before.

But in order for it to do so, she had had to accept the limitations Niall put on the relationship. That first night in her cottage had set the tone for the way things were to be. Business and pleasure were strictly defined areas, and one never mixed with the other, and as he often worked late into the evening that meant that she rarely saw him except for a belated meal.

'Wouldn't it be easier if I came to you?' she had asked one evening when he hadn't arrived at her home until ten. 'After all, I do work in Kirkham, and it would save you the long drive out.'

'I don't mind,' Niall had returned. 'It helps me wind down at the end of the day—gives me time to think——'

'About work?' Saffron couldn't erase the tart note from her voice.

'That and other things. Don't sulk, Saffron, it doesn't suit you.'

'I'm not sulking—it's just, I never see you——'

'I know, but these meetings are important.'

'Well, then——' inspiration put a gleam in her eye '—surely the people you're talking to have to eat some time. Couldn't we kill two birds with one stone?'

'No.' It was flat, emotionless, and totally decisive. 'I thought we agreed to keep our relationship private—that you didn't want people talking.'

'I know—but——'

But sometimes it seemed that Niall's insistence on privacy worked more in his favour than her own. He dictated the terms, decided when or not he could see her, and she was reduced to sitting at home, waiting for him.

'I thought you'd had enough of that with Richards—whose mama, incidentally, is still spitting acid over the way she thinks you ditched him.'

'You'd think she'd be relieved. After all, she was convinced that all I was after was the family fortune. But I suppose that, considering herself the nearest thing Kirkham has to a local aristocracy, she believes that it reflects badly on her reputation to have a mere working girl turn down her precious son and heir.'

'All the more reason not to let her know that you've replaced him with me.'

'True.' Saffron gave a faint shudder at the thought of Agnes Richards' vindictiveness if she was to find out.

'Besides——' Niall's glance at her was seductively enticing, the colour of his eyes deepening to the soft tones of antique pewter '—I much prefer it this way. In Kirkham, and at the factory, I have to be polite to so many people. When I'm here I can relax...'

His hand was sliding up her spine, stroking the delicate skin of her back, making her arch like a sensual cat.

'There's just the two of us, and I have you all to myself.'

The smile grew, becoming as warm as his caresses, drawing her to him as irresistibly as the deceptively gentle pressure of his hands.

'And that's just the way I want it. How could I ever work with you? I wouldn't be able to concentrate. When I looked at you, all I'd be able to think of would be doing this——' His mouth drifted along the side of her cheek. 'And this——'

As his lips captured hers, Saffron abandoned any thought of arguing with him further, the explosion of sensual awareness that he could set alight simply by touching her driving everything else from her mind. She loved and wanted Niall more than she had ever wanted any other man in her life and, that being so, she knew that she had no alternative but to accept his unspoken conditions, no matter how personally unsatisfactory she found them, to accept only the passionate sexual pleasure and easy companionship that was all Niall was prepared to offer, without asking for any more.

'Well, this is a surprise! I never expected to meet you here!' The unexpected sound of a man's voice jolted Saffron back to the present and she glanced up swiftly, squinting into the sun.

'Hello, Owen,' she said carefully. 'How are things with you?'

'OK.' Owen didn't sound as enthusiastic as she might have expected. 'But no thanks to that bastard Forrester. Did you know he did me out of thousands?'

'Hardly.' Saffron didn't trouble to erase the tartness from her voice. After several months away from him,

Owen sounded even more like a spoiled child to her than she remembered. 'You were asking way over the odds for the factory.'

'No more than he could afford—but, no, he'd rather spend his money on some bimbo who's caught his fancy. You didn't know about that?' he asked, seeing Saffron's start and misinterpreting the reason for it.

'I'd not heard anything.'

And she was frankly surprised that Owen had either. Niall had been so determined to keep their relationship from becoming general knowledge that they had never actually been out together in Kirkham, heading further afield for such trips to restaurants or theatres that they had been on. But the truth was that they had spent more time in Saffron's cottage—more often than not in her bed—than anywhere else.

'Oh, well, I don't expect she'll last much longer.' Owen hadn't noticed her abstracted silence. 'From what I hear, they never do. Forrester isn't noted for the length of his attachments, and Ron Bassett tells me he's not renewing the lease on his flat after September.'

Saffron managed another choked sound that might have been a response, unable to hide her relief when Owen moved on. She had forgotten that one of his friends owned the building where Niall had found a short-term let, and so, presumably, would be well aware of his future plans.

And more aware of them than she was, apparently. Niall had said nothing to her about leaving Kirkham.

Owen had barely disappeared round the corner when Niall appeared, triumphantly brandishing a bulging carrier bag.

'I found exactly what I was looking for. There's a particular historical saga my mother's deeply into—something about a Scottish adventurer in the sixteenth century—and she's been desperately hunting for volumes four and five. I got them both. Saffron?'

'Oh, sorry...' Saffron dragged her thoughts away from Owen's disturbing comments with an effort, and forced herself to switch on a bright smile. 'That's great. There's nothing worse than being part-way through something totally absorbing and not being able to find the next volume.'

'Especially when she's already bought part six—the final one—and has been struggling not to open it until she's filled in the missing bits.'

When he smiled like that her very soul lit up, Saffron thought, the sting of Owen's sneering comments easing in her heart. After all, he hadn't told her anything she didn't already know or suspect, so why should she let it get her down? But the problem was that what Owen had said had brought to the forefront of her mind something that she had been trying to avoid confronting for the past couple of weeks.

Niall's time in Kirkham wouldn't last forever. He had already spent over three months here, and according to local gossip the changes he had set in motion at Richards' were almost complete. Inevitably, sooner rather than later, he would be thinking of returning to London, and what would happen to her then?

'Why the solemn face?' Niall asked, but before Saffron could think of an answer to give him the queue moved forward suddenly and, because those in front of them wanted seats for more than two, they found themselves unexpectedly shown to the first available table, and the awkward moment passed without comment.

'I'm glad we're here and not downstairs,' Saffron said, looking around at the huge plate glass windows, decorated at the top with a stained glass design of green and gold leaves, that surrounded the ground floor of the café. 'Of course, the food is wonderful wherever you sit, but being downstairs can seem a bit enclosed.'

'Well, if you recommend this place, it must be good. I've enough experience of your cooking to value your opinion. So, tell me, what do you suggest I try?'

'Well, a Yorkshire Fat Rascal is a speciality. That's like a rich scone made with butter, spices, almonds, citrus peel and cherries. Or they do a dark and light chocolate torte that would turn a saint into a sinner. And then there are the chocolate or coffee éclairs——'

'Hang on!' Niall protested laughingly. 'You'll make it impossible to choose.'

'Then pick one for now, and we'll buy a selection of the others to take home——'

She caught herself up sharply on that revealing 'home', but luckily Niall appeared too absorbed in the menu to notice, and at that moment a smiling waitress appeared to take their order.

'I didn't think you'd be able to resist a Fat Rascal,' she commented when they were alone again. 'Though I suspected it might be a toss-up between that and the chocolate torte.'

Niall nodded, his smile a sensual curl of his lips, silver eyes gleaming wickedly.

'I'm going to follow your suggestion and take some home.' The smile grew, his eyes seeming translucent in the afternoon sunlight. 'Then I'm going to feed it to you bit by bit—while undressing you between each mouthful——'

'Niall!' Saffron whispered sharply, well aware of the fiery colour that had rushed into her cheeks. 'Behave!'

His words sounded particularly indecent in the very proper surroundings of the elegant tearooms, with the clink of china teacups and the subdued murmur of polite conversation acting as a backdrop.

'Can I help it if your beauty would turn a saint into a sinner?' he asked in mock innocence, echoing her own comment of a few moments earlier.

'Flatterer! And I very much doubt that you were ever any sort of saint!'

'Maybe not, but now that I've found those books for my mother, that's at least one person who'll consider me a candidate for canonisation. And I expect Jayne will be pleased too—she'd started on volume one the last time I saw her—— What is it?'

Disturbingly, those sharp grey eyes had caught Saffron's change of expression, the way she had shifted uncomfortably in her chair at the mention of the woman he had once cared about.

'Isn't it difficult for you to see her like that? I mean— married to your brother and pregnant with his children?'

If the roles were reversed, and she had to see Niall married to someone else, she didn't think she would be able to bear it.

'Not at all,' Niall returned calmly. 'Looking back, I don't think I ever loved Jayne at all. It was just that I got misled by the fact that she was a rare sort of woman who liked me for myself and not just for the money I earned. Anyway, as I told you, she and Andy are perfect for each other.'

'So you do believe in love for other people?' Saffron looked down at her plate to hide the pain she knew must show in her eyes.

'With my parents celebrating forty years of marriage just before Christmas I'd be a fool not to—it's just that

I've no experience of the emotion myself to judge by. In all my life I've never found anything I couldn't turn my back on in the end.'

'And just walk away.' She couldn't completely erase the uneven note from her voice. Was this a warning? Was he telling her that before too long he would turn his back on her and walk out of her life?

'Usually it's kinder that way.' The cool detachment of his tone sent an icy shiver down her spine. He sounded as if he was already halfway out of the door, mentally at least.

His tone reminded her sharply of the way he had spoken some weeks before, when, just in case she had had any doubts about the limitations he put on their relationship, he had made his position painfully clear.

'That damn place needs more work than I'd ever anticipated to get it put right, and it won't be done in a couple of weeks,' he had told her a couple of days after he had finally taken over the factory. 'I'm going to have to stay in Kirkham for much longer than I thought at first—possibly even until November.'

It had cost Saffron a great deal of effort to school her face into an expression that hid the stabbing disappointment she felt at the thought that, as always, it was business that would keep him in Kirkham, not any commitment to her.

'Will you stay at the Swan all that time?' she had asked carefully, and Niall had shaken his dark head in rejection of the idea.

'I'll have to find a temporary base somewhere for the next five months. I'm certainly not prepared to put up with hotel accommodation for that long.'

'There's always this place,' she had suggested, aiming for what she hoped was casual indifference, so that he wouldn't suspect any of the emotional baggage that went along with the offer.

For a long second he had seemed to consider the idea, but a moment later she was intensely relieved that she had made the offer sound as if it didn't matter to her one way or the other as he shook his head in firm rejection of her suggestion.

'I don't think so. I need to be nearer the factory, in case anyone wants to contact me. Somewhere in Kirkham would be better.'

Of course it would, Saffron had told herself on a wave of bitter disappointment, recognising a careful cover-up when she saw one. He wouldn't want the sort of commitment implied by moving in with her, even for a short space of time. After all, he still didn't even want their relationship to be generally known.

'Saffron?' Belatedly she became aware that Niall had spoken and she hadn't heard a word.

'I—I'm sorry——'

'I was just saying that talking of my parents has reminded me—it's Dad's birthday at the end of next week and I really should get him a present before I forget. He'd be fascinated to read about your father's work—so would Andy...'

'Is this an excuse to go back to the bookshop?' Saffron didn't know how she kept her voice so light. She even managed a smile.

'Just for a minute—five at the most—but you said you wanted to visit the Minster, so I could see you there.'

It was a good job that she had privately added an extra ten minutes to the five that Niall had promised he would be, Saffron reflected almost twenty minutes later, as she wandered around the cool, echoing aisles of the

ancient Minster. Once inside a bookshop, he completely
lost all track of time.

A sudden prickle of awareness alerted her to the fact
that she was being watched, and, looking up, she saw
the subject of her thoughts standing just inside the main
doorway, watching her with a strange, unreadable look
on his face. As soon as he realised that she had seen
him, he switched on a smile that disturbed and disconcerted her by the speed with which it came and went,
like a flashing neon sign.

'Did you get what you wanted?'

Silently Niall shook his dark head, seeming disin-
clined to speak.

'Oh, well, you'll find it somewhere else, I'm sure.'

She wasn't really surprised by his sudden silence. The
Minster had had that effect on her too, the first time she
had set foot inside it. She had felt as if her tongue had
frozen in her mouth in awe at the sight of the spectacular, soaring columns, the glorious stained glass
windows.

'It's all been beautifully restored, hasn't it? You'd
never know there'd ever been that terrible fire. Niall?'
This was more than just stunned appreciation. 'Is there
something wrong?'

He seemed to drag himself back from a long way away.

'Sorry—my mind was somewhere else.'

Somewhere none too pleasant, to judge from his expression, Saffron told herself. His eyes were clouded,
the muscles around his mouth drawn tight. But he clearly
didn't want to talk about it, and she knew it was best
not to try and probe too deeply. To do so was to risk
setting a match to the mental equivalent of a keg of gunpowder. So she confined her conversation to innocuous
facts about the Minster and the turbulent history of York

itself, finding the effort of maintaining a flow of trivial chatter harder and harder in the face of Niall's monosyllabic unresponsiveness, until finally she turned to him in exasperation as they walked down the narrow cobbled street called the Shambles.

'Have you had enough history—is that it? Because if so we might as well go home.'

'Fine,' was Niall's only response, and without another word he turned on his heel and set off towards the car park, his long stride covering the ground at such a pace that Saffron was forced to break into a trot to catch him up.

'Just what is the matter?' she demanded breathlessly as Niall bent to unlock the car.

'Matter?' he sounded as if he didn't understand what the word meant. But then a moment later he seemed to give himself another mental shake. 'Like you said—too much history.'

That smile flashed across his face again, looking even more unconvincing in the sunlight.

'I've OD'd on medieval and Roman facts,' he said brusquely, getting into the car.

Niall's silence persisted throughout the journey back to Saffron's cottage, any attempt at conversation effectively prevented by the way he put on a cassette tape of Carreras singing selections from popular operas at the sort of volume that drowned any other sound. As a result, by the time they drew up outside the tiny house, her nerves were so tightly stretched that she felt they would snap if she didn't find out soon just what was behind the uncomfortable change in his mood, even if, as she feared, it was a prelude to his breaking off their relationship.

'Are you coming in for supper? You said you wanted to watch that film on television.'

She had to ask, even though she very much suspected she knew what the answer was going to be. So much for feeding her chocolate torte bit by bit, she thought on a wave of disappointment.

'No—yes——' he corrected himself sharply. 'But nothing to eat, thanks. I couldn't manage anything after that Fat Rascal.'

For a brief moment a touch of rueful humour showed in his eyes and Saffron's heart lifted. Perhaps he'd got over whatever had annoyed him. Most likely, it was just not being able to find the book that he wanted. But when Niall dumped the bookshop carrier bag on the kitchen table, the first thing that slid out of it was an all too familiar volume.

'Dad's book! But you said——'

'Yeah—well—I was thinking of something else.'

'Obviously!'

'I saw Owen in York.'

Saffron's tart comment and Niall's quiet statement clashed in the air and then there was a sudden, taut silence during which her brain was suddenly thrown into overdrive. Was this what had put him into such a foul mood? Alarm-bells were going off inside her head.

'So did I.'

Her response was careful. She was thoroughly disconcerted by the way Niall's eyes narrowed suddenly, and he watched her closely, as if he expected her to say something more, but then abruptly his mood seemed to change.

'I'm parched—how about a drink?'

'There's lager in the fridge—and mineral water. Or I——'

'Water's fine.' He poured himself a large glassful and drank it down with obvious relish.

It *was* hot, Saffron reflected. Hot and close. The warmth of the late summer afternoon was turning to a sticky, sultry evening that seemed to threaten a coming storm.

'How's business at A Movable Feast these days?' Niall asked abruptly.

'No better. Not good—bloody awful, in fact.' The past months had seen no improvement in her financial position and things were getting close to desperate.

'Would a contract help?'

He was lounging back against one of the white-painted units, one long-fingered hand toying idly with his now empty glass, but he looked anything but relaxed. Saffron had been about to suggest that they go into the living-room and sit down, but something about his attitude made her pause. There was a tension, an aura of danger about him that made her think worryingly of the ominously dark clouds now gathering thickly on the horizon.

'Would it! You bet. You don't happen to have one hidden up your sleeve—I'll bite your hand off for it if you do.'

She wished he would look at her. It was thoroughly disconcerting trying to conduct a conversation with someone whose eyes were fixed firmly on the opposite wall.

'I've been thinking about the factory,' Niall went on inconsequentially. 'Everyone's worked damned hard on the improvements, and they deserve some sort of celebration—something everyone can join in. So, as November the fifth seems appropriate, I was thinking of a mammoth bonfire and fireworks display—open to all of Kirkham. It would combine enjoyment with some good publicity. We might even make it an annual event. We'd need food, of course—and that's where you come in.'

'You want us to do it?' All Saffron's earlier sense of constraint vanished under the rush of enthusiasm. 'Oh, yes please! Just tell me what you want. And I don't suppose you've thought about staff lunches at the factory—or at least sandwiches.' Her smile was pleading, cajoling. 'We could do those too...'

No, she'd pushed a bit too hard there—a mistake. She knew from the way Niall's face changed, the overly precise way he replaced his empty glass on the worktop. It doesn't matter—forget the idea, she was about to say, but just then Niall did look at her, and immediately she wished that he hadn't, because there was no warmth in those light eyes, only the cold, expressionless gleam of hard ice.

'Did you ever consider taking on another partner in your business—if only a sleeping one? Someone who would invest enough money to keep you afloat during this rough patch?'

Why did she suddenly feel like some small, vulnerable animal, sensing a hunter's trap but not knowing exactly where it might be?

'Well, actually, I did ask Owen if he'd consider doing just that when he sold the factory—if he got the price he wanted for it. But of course it didn't work out like that.'

No matter how hard she tried to iron out the rather breathless note in her voice, it still showed through her words. She knew that her heart was racing, not just at the hope of saving her little company, but more at the thought that if she and Niall were partners he could not just disappear out of her life.

'You could always find someone else.'

'You?' It slipped out before she could catch it back.

'Don't tell me you hadn't thought of it before now.'

Something in Niall's tone jarred, killing the rush of delight she had felt at his suggestion and replacing it with something much more uncomfortable—a cold, creeping sensation as if something slimy was crawling over her skin.

'I—had hoped...' What was the point in denying it? 'That perhaps you'd become part of my life.'

'Your business life?'

If that was all. 'Well, yes—I——'

'Of course you did,' he cut in harshly. 'After all, the money you had hoped for from Owen wasn't forth-coming—nor was the wedding-ring you were angling for—so you needed another wealthy benefactor.'

Saffron gasped in shock as the sardonic echoing of her own words hit her like a slap in the face. They had only been meant half seriously, and certainly not aimed at him, but coming from Niall they sounded like evidence for the prosecution.

'Who told you this?' she demanded sharply.

'Who do you think?' Niall flung back at her, but even as he spoke she could hear one particularly petulant voice speaking the unpleasant words.

'Owen,' she said bleakly, no room for doubt in her mind. Owen, who had made it plain that he had nothing good to say about anyone—so why should he have been any different when he had met up with Niall?

'Owen,' Niall confirmed harshly.

'And you'd believe him?' Bitterness made her voice hard. 'You never had much time for him in the past, and isn't this so obviously sour grapes?'

Unless, of course, Owen had given Niall just what he had been looking for—an excuse to turn and walk away—a reason for leaving. The thought made her feel suddenly despairingly weak.

'But Owen doesn't know he has anything to be jealous about, does he? Besides, I could have worked it out for myself. What was more obvious than that when Owen didn't come through you'd turn to someone else—someone with even more money than your little sub-urban entrepreneur? After all, what you needed was someone who was boring as hell and oily with it—someone who had nothing to recommend him but his money.'

'Oh, God!'

The cry of shock escaped her in the same moment that all colour fled from her cheeks as she recognised her own foolish words, shouted down the stairs to Kate all those weeks ago, on the day that Niall had first called at her office. He had heard them, and they had obviously stuck in his mind, festering like some open wound, until now they seemed to confirm the awful things Owen had accused her of.

'I didn't mean it quite like that——'

'No? Then how did you mean it?' His tone lashed her harshly. 'Forgive me if I find it difficult to think of any other interpretation of the words than a determination to find someone to finance you, or at the very least hand you a fortune on a plate. Are you going to deny that you took every opportunity to push your company's plight in my face?'

'N-no—but——'

'Even now, you can still think of nothing else other than some way of finding a rescue package for your damn business.' He flung the words in her face, the light-coloured eyes burning incandescent with rage. 'That's all I ever was to you, wasn't it? You're just like all the others—only after one thing——'

The pain was indescribable; she felt as if her heart was tearing slowly in two. She no longer cared whether Niall actually believed in the things he had accused her of or was simply using them as an excuse.

'Not just one thing——'

She didn't care what she was saying either, wanting only to lash out at Niall, hurt him as he was hurting her by even listening to Owen's sordid little slander.

'Though, of course, at first I didn't know that you had other skills. I never expected that we would be so good in bed together——'

She broke off sharply, silenced by his savage expletive. For a terrifying moment Niall's hands clenched into fists at his sides, but then he seemed to regain control of his temper and drew in a long, ragged breath.

'So, if I was to tell you that you haven't a hope in hell,' he said, in a voice that was so unnaturally calm that it was far more frightening than if he had shouted at her, 'that the business partnership you've been hoping for will never exist?'

'Then I'd ask you—ever so politely, of course—to stop wasting my time and get out of my life.'

If he really believed her capable of such mercenary motives, then she was better off without him. And she had always known that this moment must come sooner or later, so it was probably better to deal with it right here and now. Better a swift, sharp breaking off than a slow, agonising fraying of the fragile ties that had held them together.

'After all, you were the one who said that when something was finished it was best to go quicky, without a backward glance.'

To cover her own private pain she made her voice as cold and hard as she could, not recognising the hateful, brittle tones as her own, wanting only to drive him out, make him go so that she could break her heart in peace.

'Fine.'

She had succeeded only too well; she knew that as soon as she saw the cold gleam in those translucent eyes. His voice was icy too—freezingly, hatefully calm.

'That suits me too,' Niall said, and then he turned on his heel and strode swiftly to the door.

He didn't look back—but then, of course, she had never expected he would. But even though she had known that was how it would be, she still forced her spine to stay unnaturally stiff, willing her legs to support her, her head to lift defiantly high, until the door slammed shut behind him. Only when she knew that he had really gone, that he couldn't see her, did she let herself sink weakly into a chair, her tear-stained face in her hands.

It was supposed to hurt less if you cut something off sharply, with a single blow, she told herself despairingly. It was supposed to be much less painful than letting it wear away slowly—so why did she feel such agony? Why did she feel that there was nothing left inside her, that it had all shattered into tiny, jagged splinters? She had known that this was coming, had tried to anticipate it from the start, so why did she feel as if her world had come to a terrible, explosive end?

Because the man she loved had gone out of her life forever, and she didn't know how—or even if she could start to build up the fragmented pieces of her existence over again. In her mind, like a mockery, a nagging, throbbing ache, she heard Niall's voice saying, 'Looking back is just a waste of time...the only way is forward.' And, as if to emphasise the point, just at the moment that his car roared into life and sped off down the road, the storm which had been threatening all evening finally broke overhead, with a deafening crash of thunder and a flare of lightning that seemed to split the sky.

CHAPTER ELEVEN

THE rain that had started with the thunderstorm on the night Niall had walked out had continued almost without stopping through the following month, making the atmosphere outside as miserable and bleak as the feeling inside Saffron's heart, and now it pounded down on her head, plastering her dark hair against her skull until it hung in unflattering rats' tails around her neck and shoulders.

Miserably Saffron made a feeble attempt to wipe away the wetness from her face, heedless of the way the futile action smudged her mascara into dark panda rings around her eyes. She didn't care what she looked like anyway. Her impulsive journey to London had all been to no avail, and the house across the street from where she now stood—Niall's house—was dark and empty and securely locked. There was no one at home to respond to her desperate knock on the door.

It had been Kate who had urged her to come, persuading her against her own better instincts.

'You look dreadful,' she had said when, after days without sleep, Saffron had finally been unable to pretend any longer and had admitted to the pain that Niall's rejection had inflicted on her. 'You can't go on like this.'

'I can't do anything else,' Saffron had protested. 'Niall wants nothing more to do with me—he actually believes all that filth that Owen told him.'

'But only because you let him. You didn't even deny it—or give him a chance to say anything else.'

'Probably because there wasn't anything he wanted to say.'

But, once implanted in her mind, the doubts had taken root, proving immovable in spite of every attempt she made to drive them away. Convinced in her own mind that Niall had been preparing to end their affair, had she jumped in too quickly, pushed him into going when perhaps that hadn't been what he meant?

'You'll never know unless you ask,' had been Kate's pragmatic advice. 'Face him, Saff. Tell him why you reacted as you did. Perhaps he's feeling every bit as miserable as you.'

And Saffron had allowed herself to be persuaded, letting a tiny, weak flame of hope light up in her bruised heart. That flame had flickered slightly when, after trying to contact Niall at the factory, she had learned that he no longer lived in Kirkham but had gone back to London within twenty-four hours of walking out on her.

No backward glances. The words seemed to ring in her ears, warring with the hope she had clung to so desperately. She couldn't go back now, she knew. The only way to cope with this was to talk to Niall face to face—because there was no way this could be done over the phone.

And so she had come to London. Knowing that she didn't have the courage to set foot in the headquarters of Forrester Leisure, she had tracked down his home address by the simple expedient of forcing it out of Owen—her fury at the story he had told Niall had stunned him into handing it over without very much persuasion—and then she had taken the night train down to the capital, arriving so early in the morning that even Niall couldn't possibly be at work yet. Her heart had been beating high up in her throat, hope buzzing through her veins, as she had run up the steps to the black-painted door and pressed the bell firmly.

But there was no answer. No one had responded to her summons, no light had been switched on inside the elegant town-house, which had remained shuttered and unwelcoming as before. In the end she had had to admit that her journey had been in vain.

'You're an idiot!' she told herself fiercely when, in spite of everything, she found herself unable to leave, but lingered, miserable and uncomfortable in the steady downpour, on the opposite side of the road. 'What would a man who lives in a house like that want with a very ordinary girl like you?'

Except for the obvious, stern realism forced her to add, and she knew there was no denying it. Niall had had what he wanted from her, and now it was over.

She was finally turning away, preparing to leave, when the sound of tyres splashing down the wet street towards her made her freeze, shrinking back against the wall. There was no mistaking the sleek grey car, and her heart lurched painfully as she watched it pull up outside the house.

'Niall——'

His name escaped her lips on a whisper as her eyes went to the dark, masculine figure she so longed to see. But a moment later she could only be deeply thankful for the fact that she hadn't called it out loud or made any gesture to attract his attention as she saw that there were, in fact, two people in the car, and that the person in the driving-seat was a tall, elegant blonde who was very definitely female.

Looking back is just a waste of time. Niall's words sounded in her head like a death-knell to her foolish hopes. He certainly hadn't wasted any time that way.

She couldn't even convince herself, though she knew that
Niall was an early riser, that this scenario was more
innocent than it appeared, because as he pushed open
his door—and she was surprised to find that he *was* in
the passenger seat, the blonde actually doing the
driving—it became apparent that he was wearing evening
dress.

The elegant black jacket and trousers seemed to have
been tailored on to his lithe form, and the whiteness of
his shirt formed a stark contrast to the jet darkness of
his hair. At some point he had dragged off his bow tie
and loosened the top couple of buttons of his shirt—or
the blonde had done that for him—Saffron reflected bitterly, recognising an uncharacteristically rumpled edge
to Niall's appearance that brought her hard up against
the painful but unavoidable possibility that he had un-
dressed earlier and then hastily and none too carefully
pulled on his clothes again in order to make the journey
home.

Huddled into a corner, trying desperately to become
invisible, Saffron heard Niall's low voice as it carried
clearly across the silent street, the unmistakable note of
intimate warmth in his words stabbing like a brutal knife
into her already wounded heart.

'Are you sure you won't come in for coffee—or anything else?'

The blonde's reply was indistinct, though obviously
negative, but Saffron caught the warmth in her voice
that softened her refusal.

'Besides,' she added more clearly as Niall swung his
long legs on to the glistening tarmac, 'you need to
get into bed. After a night like last night, you'll need
some sleep.'

'You too,' Niall retorted laughingly, the implication
of his words burning like bitter acid in Saffron's mind,
and she was grateful for the hot tears that stung her eyes,
blurring the image of his dark head lowering to press a
farewell kiss on the woman's cheek. 'I'll be round to
collect the car this evening. Take care, Jay, love—drive
safely.'

Through a haze of misery Saffron heard the car door
slam and Niall's hurried footsteps running up the steps
to his door, where he paused to wave after the departing
car.

If she kept absolutely still, she told herself, then
perhaps he wouldn't notice her. It was barely light, and
the gloom of the rain, her black coat, might just conceal
her. But in the end her own weakness betrayed her. She
couldn't stop herself from turning her head, couldn't
resist the temptation to take one last bittersweet look at
his beloved face, the long, lean lines of his body as he
stood in his doorway.

That tiny movement was her downfall. Catching it out
of the corner of his eye, Niall swiftly turned his attention in her direction, those steely grey eyes, almost
the same colour as the rain-clouds above them, fixing
on her face with a laser-like intensity that she could feel
even across the street which separated them.

For a long, long moment, he froze, staring at her, and
she could have sworn that his lips moved, forming the
sound of her name, and that he took a single step
forward—towards her. But then abruptly he stopped,
shaking his head so hard that it sent that errant lock of
jet-black hair flying forward on to his forehead as it had
done so often in the past.

But this time there was no hope that he would let her
brush it back; she knew that in the moment that his ex-

pression changed, his face hardening before he turned
from her, thrusting his key into the lock with a haste
that revealed only too clearly how keen he was to get
away from her. The sound of the glossy black door
slamming shut behind him drove the point home like a
brutal blow in her face. He had made his decision, and
she knew she had no hope of appeal.

So now she knew. The tiny hope was gone, killed off
once and for all by the hard-faced indifference he had
shown her. Niall didn't want her. He had found someone
else, someone with whom he had obviously just spent a
very intimate and satisfying night. He might have wanted
her once, and, true to his declaration, had gone straight
for what he wanted—but he had also warned her how
he would react when he grew bored.

This was the second time he had shown her that he
had meant what he said, that he was perfectly capable
of turning his back and walking away without looking
back. She wasn't so much of a fool that she needed the
message driving home any more forcefully. With desperate tears blending into the raindrops on her cheeks,
she turned and ran stumblingly away.

The sound of her doorbell ringing on and on dragged
Saffron from the heavy sleep of exhaustion into which
she had fallen an hour or so before. At least, she had
thought it was only an hour—two at the most—but a
hasty glance at her alarm clock told her that it was, in
fact, eight times that. Worn out by the stress of recent
weeks, her body had finally succumbed to the need for
the oblivion that had escaped it for so long.

'Go away!' she groaned, putting her fingers into her
ears to drown out the sound, but the childish action failed
to obliterate the persistent noise, and suddenly remem-

bering that she had promised to ring Kate as soon as possible, to let her know what had happened, she was overcome with guilt at the thought that her friend had probably called round in a state of some concern.

'All right—I'm coming!'

Snatching up her white towelling dressing-gown, she stumbled downstairs, eyes still blurred with sleep, her hair a tangled mess, and unlocked the door in a rush.

'Kate—I'm sorry. But honestly there's nothing to report. I saw Niall and——'

The words died on her lips as her gaze focused on the tall, dark, very masculine form of the last person she had expected to see—and he was very definitely *not* Kate.

'You saw Niall, and——?' he drawled sardonically. 'So it *was* you.'

'Of course it was!' His change of tone on the last four words bothered her. She couldn't interpret what lay behind it. 'You know it was—you saw me.'

The pain of that moment stabbed at her again, and acting on a purely reflex action she made a move to slam the door shut in his face. But Niall anticipated her response, blocking the movement by the simple expedient of ramming one booted foot hard up against the door and wedging it open.

'I didn't realise—not at first. I'd had a—very heavy night, and I wasn't thinking at all straight. I really thought that I was seeing things—that I was still drunk.'

'You really know how to make me feel small!' Saffron flung at him bitterly. 'You thought I was just a figment of your intoxicated imagination!'

'I was inside the house before I started thinking clearly, and when I looked again you'd gone. Look, do you think you could let me in, just for a minute? I'm getting soaked out here.'

Niall's sudden appearance seemed to have fogged her brain. She hadn't even noticed that it was raining again, the same sort of steady downpour that had drenched her the day before. Niall's hair was already wet, flattened to his skull in a way that reminded her painfully of so many occasions when she had seen him fresh from taking a shower—or sharing one with her.

It would serve him right if she left him outside, or turned away from him as he had done to her, she told herself, but something in his face, a strangely diffident expression that was quite unlike the Niall she knew, twisted something sharply in her too-vulnerable heart.

'Please——' Niall had seen the change in her face.

'Well...'

'Oh, come on, Saffron, surely it's better to talk in comfort. Besides, you'll freeze if you stay there much longer, dressed like that.'

Saffron gave a shocked gasp as Niall's words brought home to her the fact of her half-dressed state. Frozen in shock at the sight of him on her doorstep, she now realised that she still had only one arm in the dressing-gown's sleeve—the other was hanging loose at her back. The robe itself hung open, revealing her short yellow satin nightdress to his coldly appraising gaze. Hastily she pulled the white towelling round her, shoving her hand into the sleeve and belting the robe firmly around her slim waist.

'You'd better come in,' she muttered ungraciously, pushing a nervous hand through the tangled mane of her dark hair in a vain attempt to restore it to some sort of order. 'I'll make some coffee.'

She could do with a drink herself, she reflected as she filled the kettle and switched it on. It might make her brain start functioning at last. She had just registered fully exactly what Niall must have meant by a 'heavy night' and it brought a foul taste into her mouth.

'Why were you there?' Niall asked suddenly. 'What did you come all the way to London for?'

'I could ask the same of you,' Saffron told him sharply, distracting herself by collecting mugs, tea-spoons, coffee-granules and milk from the fridge as she spoke. 'After all, you can't expect me to believe that you've driven a couple of hundred miles to Kirkham simply to find out what I wanted when you could just have picked up a phone.'

He must have left almost as soon as he had sobered up—once he'd collected his car from the beautiful Jay. The thought of the elegant blonde was a slash of pain that had her hand clenching on the neck of the milk bottle.

'Why did you come?' Niall ignored her tirade.

'Perhaps I wanted to see how the other half lives.'

No, flippancy was a definite mistake; Niall's dark scowl told her that. He looked tired, she thought re-gretfully, pale and drained, with shadows under those spectacular eyes. His jaw was dark with the day's growth of beard, and the black T-shirt and jeans he wore under a loose denim jacket seemed to emphasise the fact. Probably worn out by too many 'heavy nights', she told herself tartly, pushing away the weak sympathy that had tried to sneak into her mind.

'Actually, I wanted to talk to you about Bonfire Night.' She took refuge behind the excuse she had thought up as an explanation for her presence in London if she had managed to speak to him.

'What about Bonfire Night?'

Saffron drew a deep breath and brought it out in a rush. 'I think you'd better get someone else to do the catering.'

'Why the hell should I do that?' Niall demanded harshly.

'Isn't it obvious?'

'Not to me.' He was being deliberately awkward. 'We had a contract——'

'An agreement only—and that was before we—you——'

'Our personal lives have no bearing on this what-soever.' She couldn't believe how cold and distant his voice was, and his eyes were as bleak and unrevealing as the North Sea on a winter's day. 'And I happen to think that your company will be perfect for the sort of thing I want.'

'Well, I won't do it! I can't. A Movable Feast is going out of business—I'm closing it down.'

'You'd do that rather than work for me?'

'It's not a question of choice, damn you!'

It was as if she had slapped him hard in the face. Niall took a step backwards, his hard features losing colour, his eyes clouding.

'You——God, Saffron, I never wanted that!'

'It's not your fault!' Saffron put in swiftly, driven by strict honesty. 'It's this damned recession—there just isn't the business out there.'

'But have you tried advertising—a leaflet campaign? You could——'

'Niall, please!' Saffron's voice was thick and choked. She found it an unbearably bitter irony that when he had once been so determined to have nothing to do with her business, now he was apparently keen to help. 'I've tried everything I can think of and I can see no way out.'

Suddenly, belatedly, she became aware of the way that the rainwater was dripping from his hair, falling in damp patches onto his jacket and the T-shirt beneath it, flattening it against the strong lines of his chest, reminding her of how, in the past, she had peeled it off him . . .

'Oh, for heaven's sake!' Exasperation hid the other, more complicated feelings in her voice. 'Take that jacket off and hang it near the boiler—it'll dry out there. And get a towel to see to your hair.'

The kettle boiled while he did as he was told, and she was grateful for the fact that he had his back to her because it meant that he didn't see the way her hand shook as she reached for it.

'About the business—I could——'

'No!' Saffron couldn't bear to let him continue. 'You can't do anything because I won't accept anything from you. I—— Oh, no!'

She broke off on a cry of pain as the kettle swung in her unsteady grip and boiling water splashed over her hand.

'Saffron!'

Reacting with instinctive speed, Niall pulled her towards the sink, wrenching on the cold tap as he did so. Saffron gave a shaky sigh of relief as the icy water poured on to her hand, soothing the pain of her injured fingers. In spite of her efforts to hold them back, a couple of weak tears slid from the corners of her eyes and trickled down her cheeks.

'Oh, God, Saffron!' Niall said, in a new and very different tone, one that shattered what little was left of her peace of mind, the unexpected thread of concern rocking her belief in his total indifference to her feelings.

'It doesn't hurt so much now,' she managed unevenly, and had no idea, even in her own mind, whether she meant her scalded hand or the cruelty of his rejection of her.

She wished that he would move away, or that she had never told him to take off his jacket. His nearness, the feel of that muscular body so close to hers, firm and hard underneath the clinging softness of his T-shirt, was almost more than she could bear. She could breathe in the scent of him with a sensuality that was almost shocking, the soft sound of his breathing played havoc with her already sensitive nerves and the temptation to lean back against him, feel those strong arms enfold her, was only just resistible.

'Saffron...' Niall said, and his voice had changed once again. This time there was a suggestion of hesitation, something she might almost have described as tentativeness, that was so unexpected it made her turn stunned brown eyes on his face, only to find that once she had met the smoky force of his heavy-lidded gaze she couldn't look away again.

He was going to kiss her, she told herself. He wanted to kiss her, and she, weak fool that she was, was going to let him, because she couldn't resist him. She had never had the strength to hold out against the sexual appeal of his beautiful male body, the strongly carved features of his face, the startling contrast of the softness of his hair.

One kiss, she told herself. Just one, and then she'd put a stop to this.

But she'd reckoned without the physical fireworks, the explosive detonation that simply touching Niall could set off in her body, every nerve suddenly seeming electrically charged. Behind her, the water gushed unheeded into the sink, completely forgotten as she swayed against him, her mouth opening softly to allow the tantalising enticement of his tongue.

'Saffron, sweetheart,' he murmured against her lips. 'Why do we let other things get in the way of this——?'

He should never have spoken. The sound of his voice, touched with the same husky warmth that had shaded it when he spoke to the blonde in his car, slashed through the haze of delight that was clouding her senses, and when his hands moved over her body, pushing the white robe aside, reminding her of how little she had on, she snapped back to reality with a jarring suddenness, jerking backwards as his fingers moved to slide the delicate lacy straps of her nightdress down over her shoulders.

'*No!*' Her hands pushed frantically at his hard chest. 'Niall—I said no!'

'Saffron, honey, you don't mean that.'

He was using the snake-charmer's voice again, effortlessly weaving a spell around her mind in the same way that his kisses, his touch, had enchanted her body.

'We both know what this leads to—how good it can be——'

'No!'

With a movement that wrenched at her heart as much as her body, she tore herself away from him. On the day they had first met, at the restaurant, she had thought of the yearning he could awaken in her in the form of a coiled, sleeping snake, and now she saw that, as with a real serpent, awakening her sexuality had created something that was both beautiful and dangerous. Her desire for Niall had been a source of great delight at first, but blinded by that pleasure she had been unable to see that its bite was in fact lethally destructive in the way that it weakened her, putting her at his mercy.

'I can't believe you're such a sexual opportunist—that you'd try it on in this way. What about your new woman—the one I saw you with—your blonde——?'

'My blonde?'

Suddenly, amazingly, he was laughing, his dark head thrown back, silver eyes gleaming in genuine amusement. 'Oh, God, Saffron, this is such a cliché! That was Jayne.'

'Jayne?' The name rang faint bells, but she couldn't quite remember...

'My sister-in-law. The one who got away and married my brother. If you'd been able to see into the car properly you'd have realised how pregnant she is.'

Saffron's head was spinning. 'But how—why?'

'I'd been to a dinner party with Andy and Jayne. During the evening I—I drank more than was wise, and very sensibly Jayne refused to let me drive home. She even confiscated my keys so that I had to spend what little was left of the night in their spare bedroom. Then, in the morning, because she knew I was still not one hundred per cent, she drove me home and, being the determined lady she is, held on to my car until *she* was sure I was fit to drive.'

'It must have been one hell of a night.'

'Believe me, it was,' Niall admitted wryly. 'So you see, sweetheart, you don't have to worry about Jayne.'

He meant the words to be reassuring and, on the surface at least, they were. But it was hearing them in that dismissive tone that brought home to Saffron just why she really *did* have to worry.

'Oh, but I do.'

Jayne might not matter in the present, but it was what she had been to Niall in the past that made her so important. He had believed himself to be in love with Jayne, but when she had chosen his brother instead he had had no trouble in getting over that awkward feeling and moving on. 'It was how little it bothered me that was worrying,' he had said, and she would be more than wise to take warning from that now.

'You walked out on me once, Niall; how long before you do so again? Do you have another brother you can pass me on to when you grow tired?'

'It won't be like that——'

'No, it won't, because I'm not going to let it happen. I'm not prepared to go through that again.'

'You won't have to——'

Niall reached out and drew her close again, his lips on her face, trailing burning kisses over the soft skin of her cheek, down the slender line of her throat, coming perilously close to the pale curves exposed by the deeply scooped neckline of her nightdress.

'I said *no*!'

It took all her strength to say it, all her courage to look into his face and see those clear eyes cloud over in genuine confusion and disbelief. He had been so sure of himself—of her. He had never imagined that she might actually turn him down.

'You might be able to dismiss those ugly accusations you flung at me, but I can never forget that you believed them in the first place. I thought you hated me because I was only after your money.'

Niall's shrug dismissed her objection with a lack of concern that further convinced her she had made the right decision.

'Would you believe, I don't care any more?'

'Oh, yes. I can believe that only too easily. You can forget them *now*, when it suits you. You can dismiss them just like that.'

A dreary, deadly sense of despair told her that in just this way would he dismiss *her* when he decided he had had enough.

'The fireworks you said we lit between us might be enough for you to compensate for such a lack of trust—they might even have made a brilliant display at first.'

And she could hardly deny that with her body aching, yearning, needing his touch so desperately. Drawing a deep, uneven breath, she forced herself to ignore the physical pain, concentrating instead on the mental one.

'But, like all pyrotechnics, they have only a very temporary glory. As far as I'm concerned, they've burned themselves out, leaving only a blackened, smoking stub!'

'You don't mean that——'

'Oh, yes, I do!'

Resolutely ignoring the protest from every nerve, the agonising pain in her heart, she wrenched herself away and struggled to restore some order to her appearance, hampered by the way she seemed to have lost control over her hands.

'And I mean this even more—you may say that you don't care, but I do. I care that you even thought I was capable of something so low, so despicable! So, let me tell you something once and for all, Mr Wealthy Benefactor Forrester! I don't want your money, or your influence, or your help. I don't want your company, or your—lovemaking.'

The word threatened to destroy her control, sticking in her throat and almost choking her, but she forced it out with a ruthless determination that she hadn't known she possessed.

'I don't want *you*! So will you please get out of my life and leave me alone? I never want to see you again!'

For one dreadful moment she thought that he was going to refuse to go. His face had closed up, his eyes becoming blank and dead, as if steel shutters had slammed shut behind them, and the muscles around his mouth and jaw were drawn tight over the strong bones. But then he gave a curt nod and moved deliberately away from her.

'I'll go, Saffron,' he said, and the terrible coldness of his voice seemed to freeze the blood in her veins. 'For now. But I won't leave you alone. You see, I want you to provide the food for the Bonfire Night celebrations, and I won't have anyone else.'

'You can't force me!'

'No, I can't.' The mildness of his agreement was somehow more frightening than if he had raged at her. 'But if you won't do it, no one else will. I'll cancel the whole thing.'

'Oh, but you can't do that!' Saffron was appalled. 'It's already been announced. Everyone in Kirkham's looking forward to it. All the children are so excited— you can't disappoint them!'

'I can and I will, unless you fulfil your part of the bargain,' Niall stated inflexibly. 'It won't do you any harm—it might even do some good. Think of it as a publicity venture—a last-ditch attempt to save A Movable Feast.'

She couldn't find a word to say, either to agree or refuse. He was just using this to torment her, perhaps in some cruel way to get back at her for damaging his macho pride by turning him down. She couldn't really have any hope that all the publicity in the world would finally drag her business out of the swamp of near-bankruptcy.

'What about Kate and your other workers? Don't they deserve one last attempt to save their jobs—their livelihood?'

'You really know how to twist the knife,' Saffron flung at him bitterly. It would always be on her conscience if she took Kate and the others down with her.

'Oh, come on, Saffron! Is it really so very much to ask? You co-operate with me on this for just a few short weeks, and before you know it I'll be gone—back to London—leaving you in peace.'

Privately, Saffron doubted that the future held any sort of peace for her, whether Niall was here or in London. Loving him the way she did, and knowing that he felt only a temporary physical desire for her, had drained all light, all joy from her life.

'Well—will you do it? Or do I cancel the event?' Niall demanded harshly.

Which, of course, left her with only one possible reply. He had her in a cleft stick, and he was well aware of that fact.

'You don't leave me any choice,' she said resignedly. 'You know I have to do it.'

CHAPTER TWELVE

'SAUSAGES—hundreds of them—rolls, baked potatoes...'

Saffron ticked off items on her check-list as each carefully packed box was carried from the kitchen into the waiting van.

'Gingerbread men—sorry—gingerbread *persons*! Toffee apples... Kate, I thought there were going to be more——'

'Right here!' Her friend's voice was calm and reassuring. 'Don't panic. Everything's under control.'

With regard to the food, at least, that was true, Saffron thought unhappily. If only the rest of her life could be as easily organised and positive. Instead it seemed to be falling to pieces around her, and there was nothing she could do to stop it.

She didn't really know how she had got through the past five weeks. Once she had agreed to provide the food for the bonfire, she had thought that Niall would then leave her strictly alone to do just that, while he concentrated on the other details. She had also assumed that he wouldn't be staying in Kirkham any longer than he actually had to, but would spend most of his time in London, sending instructions by telephone or fax, and only appearing on the big day itself, when his presence as the new owner of Richards' Rockets would naturally be required, and that as a result she wouldn't see very much of him.

She couldn't have been more wrong. At times it now seemed that she was in his company more than she had ever been when they had been together. Certainly, she was seen more often in public with him.

For some reason, Niall seemed to have appointed her not only to the position of caterer, but also consultant on all matters relating to the likes and dislikes of the people of Kirkham, so that, no matter how much she protested, she was always being roped in to give her opinion on the choice of music, the design of the displays—anything at all. He also seemed to change his mind about the food to be provided with a frequency that both infuriated and bewildered her, and had the circumstances been different, and Niall just an ordinary client, she would have handed in her notice and walked away without hesitation.

But Niall was no ordinary client, and because he was who he was, the very existence of the Bonfire Night celebrations depended on her. She could have no doubt that if she backed out Niall would carry out his threat to cancel everything, and as the days passed and the excitement grew she knew she could never let that happen. And so she pushed to one side the ill-effects of nights without sleep, the lack of appetite that kept her from eating, tacked a wide, bright smile on to her face and forced herself to endure the torment of days spent with Niall in an existence that brought home to her the true, bitter meaning of 'so near and yet so far'.

'That's the lot.' Kate sighed with relief. 'It's been a mammoth task, but we've done it. We can certainly pat ourselves on the back this time. And its done us no harm on the business front, either—all that publicity for one thing. We'll be raking in the profits soon.'

'Maybe.' Saffron smiled rather wanly at her friend's enthusiasm. 'It's a little too early to be counting any chickens yet, let alone any profits. But all the free advertising has helped get our name known.'

She had to admit that Niall had been more than fair in the way that he had made sure that every poster, every hand-out, every newspaper report on the coming event always featured the words, 'Catering by A Movable Feast' displayed in a prominent position. As a result, there had been a sudden rush of interest in her business that had given a much-needed boost to her hopes of keeping it going after all.

'And perhaps we'll take some more orders tonight. We've got a lot to thank your Niall for.'

'Not *my* Niall,' Saffron corrected automatically.

'Still no chance of making up?' Kate enquired gently, and Saffron shook her head, her unhappiness showing on her face.

'I realised I'm not cut out for a temporary affair, after all. I am like my sisters, Kate; I do need love and marriage, or at least commitment—I can't settle for less.'

'Not even for Niall Forrester?'

Particularly not for Niall Forrester, Saffron thought later that evening as she watched Niall ceremonially set light to the enormous bonfire that had been built in the middle of a huge field on the outskirts of the town. If Niall loved her, she would go through hell and high water for him; she would probably not even ask for the commitment she had said she wanted, but take each day at a time and be content with that—if he loved her.

But she knew that his relationship with her had come under the heading of things he wanted, nothing more, and, loving him the way she did, that would never be enough. She couldn't live her life with a man who didn't trust her, who had wanted to keep their relationship hidden, driving home his emotional independence from her by setting up a completely separate home, turning down her offer to share her cottage. He hadn't even known how much that offer had cost her. With a sigh she turned away, and tried to concentrate her attention on the huge trestle tables laden with food.

'Everything OK?'

Niall had come up behind her, his casual question making her jump nervously.

'Fine.' She fiddled unnecessarily with a pile of napkins, unable to make herself look at him, afraid of what her own face might reveal.

'You've done a brilliant job——' She sensed rather than saw the tilt of his dark head that indicated the display of food. 'There's enough here to feed several armies and still have plenty to take home. You managed to get all the extra staff you needed?'

Saffron nodded silently, still keeping her face averted.

'There were plenty of wives and girlfriends of the factory workers who were only too willing to help.'

'And the sweatshirts were all right?'

'They were fabulous!' Genuine delight overcame the rigid restraint she was imposing on her voice and she swung round in a gesture of spontaneous enthusiasm, a smile breaking through her control.

It had been Niall's suggestion that the women who staffed the refreshment tables should wear some sort of uniform, and he had taken it on himself to have sweatshirts made in an assortment of colours, all decorated with an attractive print of a picnic basket filled to overflowing, and the words 'A Movable Feast' in clear, white lettering. She was wearing one of them now, the rich, golden yellow a foil for her dark hair and pale skin.

'It was a brilliant idea! Thank you for...'

Her voice trailed off, her stomach lurching painfully as she realised that, without thinking, she had caught hold of Niall's arm to emphasise her point.

For the first time since he had come up to her, she looked directly at Niall, her breath catching in her throat as she saw the way his strong profile was etched against the firelight, the flames casting flickering, changeable shadows across the hard bones and planes of his face, their glow reflected warmly in the pale depths of his eyes. Like her, he was dressed casually, aiming for comfort and warmth in jeans and a rich blue sweater, and as her eyes dropped nervously to where her fingers encircled the strength of his arm she had a sudden agonising recollection of just how it had felt to be held in those arms, to feel them close around her... With a wordless sound of distress, she snatched her hand away again, reacting as sharply as if she had been burned by the heat of his skin.

'My pleasure.' Niall's tone was dry, so much so that she wasn't exactly sure that he was referring to her comment about the sweatshirts. 'They should help to get the name of your business known anyway—all good publicity.'

'We've certainly had plenty of that,' she told him, struggling to impose some degree of control on her voice. 'The advertising has resulted in all sorts of enquiries. We've got a couple of definite contracts and plenty of interest.'

'I'm glad.' Niall's voice was low and slightly husky. 'I've tried every damn thing I could think of to put custom your way.'

'*You* have!' Saffron turned wide, startled brown eyes on his shadowed face. 'Why?'

'I wanted to make sure that you didn't lose your business.'

'You did that? For me?'

'It was the only way I could be sure that you wouldn't need me as a partner.'

Behind Saffron's back a newly lit rocket soared upwards into the pitch-black sky, exploding with a shriek into a hail of multicoloured stars, and she could only be thankful that the way that the unexpected sound had made her jump like a startled cat had hidden the agonising distress that had stabbed home at Niall's words.

He still didn't trust her. He still thought that her only interest in him was financial, that all she had ever wanted from him was a rescue package for A Movable Feast.

'Well, you've certainly managed that.'

The moment's respite had given her a chance to impose a rigid control on her voice, and she was relieved to find that it sounded reasonably light-hearted, even though deep inside she felt as if she was breaking up, shattering into tiny, desolate fragments.

'And now I suppose you think I should be suitably grateful?'

'Grateful? Why the hell should you be grateful? Look—I know you wanted to sort things out on your own, and all I've done is simply point people in your direction. *You're* the one who's impressed them enough to want to employ you. The way you've tackled the catering for tonight is evidence enough of your flair and efficiency. That's why people have decided to use A Movable Feast, not because of any pressure from me.'

Saffron found it hard to believe what she was hearing. If Niall had understood her double-edged use of the word 'grateful', then obviously he had deliberately ignored it, instead offering her the sort of unpatronising praise that any human being would love to hear, and that sent a warm glow through her bruised heart.

'I have something for you.'

Saffron stared at the white envelope Niall had pulled from his pocket, eyeing it warily, as if it was a rat that might bite.

'Take it—you've earned it.'

Saffron's hands were slightly unsteady as she ripped the letter open, but even before she had fully unfolded the single sheet of paper it enclosed she knew with a sense of distress just what it was. And she was right. There before her, perfectly typed and formally spelled out, was an offer to employ A Movable Feast to provide business lunches at Richards' Rockets...

She read no further, but, screwing the letter up into a tight, crumpled ball, marched determinedly towards the fire and flung it as far from her as she could, watching with intense satisfaction the swift flare of flame that devoured it.

'I know exactly how it feels,' Niall murmured behind her. 'You have just that effect on me, too.'

'*What*?'

Not knowing whether she was furious or flattered, Saffron whirled round, her dark hair flying.

'What are you trying to do to me, Niall?' she demanded. 'You bully me into doing the food for this damn bonf——'

'Yes, I know. I'm sorry about that, but it was the only thing I could think of.'

Niall's voice was disturbingly different, and his expression was as penitent as his tone. Blinking hard in shock, Saffron stared into his eyes, seeing the flicker of the fire reflected in them, the changing shadows suddenly making him look so unlike the man she thought

she knew, the confident, controlled, ruthless Niall
Forrester she had first met.

'And—and then you try to bribe me——'

'No, not bribe,' Niall cut in sharply. 'I told you—you'd
earned it. And the letter—the contract didn't come from
me. I've put a manager in charge at Richards'—a good
man...'

He didn't need to go on. In her mind, Saffron could
see the letter as clearly as if it was before her eyes, and
even in the brief survey she had given it she had sub-
consciously absorbed the fact that it had not been Niall's
firm slash of a signature at the bottom of the type-
written page.

'But he does as you say——'

'It's his opinion that counts on local matters, Saffron.
I don't have time to attend to every last little detail for
all my companies—that's what I employ a manager for.'

He couldn't have used an argument more guaranteed
to convince her. Did she really think that Niall Forrester,
head of Forrester Leisure, would bother about trivial
matters like who cooked his employees' lunches?

'So, you've finished your job here.' Saffron's heart
twisted at the thought that his words were also evidence
of just how much Niall was moving away from Kirkham.

'Richards' is up and running, yes.'

'You'll be heading back to London...'

'There's one more thing I have to see to first. Saffron,
I have something else for you.'

A new tension in the long powerful body before her,
the way a muscle moved in his jaw, alerted her to the
fact that this was something very different from the
business contract.

'I don't want——' she began, but Niall brushed her
protest aside.

'But, believe me, if you throw this in the fire, then I'll go right in after it.'

'You'll——' The husky intensity in his voice frightened her. 'What do you mean?'

'Saffron——'

Niall broke off suddenly, interrupted by a sound that began as a sort of intrigued murmur, then grew in volume and strength, gathering force like a wave rushing in to the shore. His eyes went to something behind Saffron's back, and a look of shock and consternation crossed his face.

'Oh, God!' he muttered. 'Damn them—I said nine-thirty. Saffron——'

The noise around them was increasing so quickly that she could hardly hear Niall speak, and then, slowly, through the din and confusion, she became aware that everyone was shouting a single word—her own name.

'Saffron! *Saffron*!'

'What is it?'

Spinning round in response, she was momentarily dazzled by the flare of light from a huge set-piece firework display erected at the far end of the field, slightly raised above the rest so that no one could miss it.

'Saffron——' Niall said again, a touch of desperation in his voice, but by now her vision had cleared, so that she could focus properly—though when she realised what was before her she had to doubt whether she was, in fact, seeing what was really there or just imagining things.

MARRY ME, SAFFRON!

The huge, brilliant letters blazed out of the night sky, spelling out their message for everyone to see.

Marry me, Saffron! Her brain reeled in shock. It couldn't be true; she was imagining things.

Dazedly she turned back to Niall, seeing the strain on his face, the hand he had taken from his pocket, the tiny, square jeweller's box on his palm . . .

'You—— But—— *You*!'

Silently he nodded, his eyes never leaving her face.

'You—— You did that?'

'It wasn't supposed to be set off until I'd had a chance to ask you privately,' he said hurriedly. 'And it was meant to say *please*—but obviously one of the damn fuses didn't light properly.'

To Saffron's astonished eyes he looked suddenly very boyish, impossibly young, and disturbingly vulnerable.

'Saffron! Saffron?'

The crowd was calling her name. Friendly faces were all around her, eyes gleaming with curiosity in the firelight.

'Saffron—tell us. What's your answer?'

She could only turn to Niall, unable to speak, even to think. Her face had lost all colour and her brown eyes were just dark pools of shock.

'Oh, God!' Niall's exclamation was low and harsh and he caught hold of her arm in a grip that bruised. 'Let's get out of here!'

Dazedly Saffron let him lead her away, his arm coming round her waist, drawing her close into the protective warmth of his body. She was vaguely aware of the light touch with which he parried questions, deflected curious bystanders, answered laughing comments, but couldn't make herself focus on anything. All around her the noise of the celebrations, the crash and fizz of fireworks, the crackle of the fire, the murmur of the crowds, seemed to blur into a whirling, multicoloured haze.

And then at last they were well away from the fire,
and suddenly it was quiet, and very dark, and there was
only the two of them. Sure-footed on the uneven grass,
Niall led her across the field to the deserted spot where
his car was parked, releasing her only to unlock the door.

Still too numbed to think for herself, Saffron let herself
be manoeuvred into the front seat and waited in silence,
staring straight in front of her, until Niall moved round
to the driver's side and got in beside her. The slam of
the car door cut off the last traces of sound from outside,
enclosing them in their own private world.

After a long silent moment Niall moved to switch on
the reading light above them before turning to take both
her hands in his.

'Saffron—I'm sorry. I should have thought. I didn't
mean——'

Didn't mean——! Pain seared through Saffron at his
words. What was this, then? Some sick, cruel joke?

'I didn't think. I just wanted to do something spectacular to show you how much I love you, but I should
have realised——'

Saffron stirred at last, her trance shattered by the sight
of Niall Forrester, a man she had never known at a loss
for words, suddenly fumbling for them, stumbling over
each phrase. And *had* he said——?

'Love?' she croaked, and at the sound of her voice
Niall froze into sudden stillness then, with a swift, muttered curse, pushed rough hands through the black
sleekness of his hair.

'I'm doing this all wrong—I'm sorry. I should have
told you that first, but the man I left in charge of the
firework display obviously got itchy fingers——'

'Tell me now.'

That stopped him dead. He looked at her, silver eyes touched with doubt, then drew a deep, ragged breath.

'Saffron Ruane, I love you,' he stated, so slowly and clearly that there could be no possible doubt as to exactly what he had said.

'But you don't believe in love.'

'Didn't believe,' he corrected gently. 'And that was quite simply because I'd never experienced it. I might have thought I knew about it, and perhaps I came close with the way I felt about Jayne, but I only cared about her as much as I could for a potential sister-in-law, not someone with whom I wanted to spend the rest of my life.'

'You could still walk away.' Saffron's voice was low and uncertain, but he caught it and nodded slowly, his expression serious.

'But I can't walk away from you. I tried it once and it almost destroyed me.'

'And yet you believed Owen——'

'No—yes—— Sweetheart, I feel so bad about that. I can only say that I was so off-balance I didn't really know what I was doing. I'd already realised that I was in so deep—deeper than I'd ever been before—that, quite honestly, it scared me. I'd never let anything have that much control over me before. I'd built myself a world that I liked—one that worked perfectly—and suddenly it was all turned upside-down and I wasn't in the driving-seat any more. Then Richards came along with his vicious tongue, like the serpent in the Garden of Eden——'

He broke off abruptly, shaking his dark head as if in despair at his own behaviour.

'I didn't want to believe him—I *shouldn't* have believed him—but I'd been there before. I'd had my fill of women who were only interested in my money. I wanted to believe you weren't like that, but there were so many things you'd said, and the thought that *you* could do that to me blew me right off-course. I couldn't think straight—and when I challenged you——'

'The way I reacted seemed to confirm what Owen had said,' Saffron put in sombrely. 'I was so convinced that you were preparing to leave me that I didn't even bother to fight.' She had given him a push out of the door, in fact. 'I behaved like the person you thought I was.'

'Exactly—and I couldn't forget our first meeting——'

Saffron groaned aloud, colour flaring in her cheeks. She could just imagine how she had seemed to him.

'That was such a mistake—but I was so angry. I wanted to shock Owen. Instead, I shocked you, appearing to be bold and mercenary, brittle and demanding, just like the person I pretended to be when you told me what Owen had said. It was all just a front,' she said sadly. 'I'm sorry—I must have hurt you.'

'And made me mad as hell,' Niall admitted ruefully. 'So mad I couldn't think straight for weeks. I took off to London because I told myself I couldn't bear to be in the same town as you, but I felt as if I'd been torn in two. It was as if we weren't two separate people any more, as if we'd fused together to form a sort of third entity—something stronger—bigger—more beautiful than we could ever be on our own. And without you I was less than half a person.'

For a man who hadn't believed in love, he'd just given an incredibly powerful description of that emotion, Saffron thought dazedly, tears of joy pricking at her eyes.

'That was why you saw me with Jayne——'

The grin Niall turned on her was boyishly shamefaced.

'I was losing my grip on things, and at that damn dinner party I was drinking to try to forget about you. I ended up completely out of my head—so much so that Jay decided to take me in hand. She sat me down and listened while I poured everything out—we talked until five the next morning. When I'd finished she gave me her advice—to get myself sobered up and get back to you as quickly as possible to sort things out. You were so much on my mind—that was why I thought I was seeing things when I got out of the car and there you were. And when I realised it hadn't been my imagination and looked again you'd gone.'

He shuddered violently, remembering, and Saffron twisted her hand in his until she was holding him, squeezing his fingers tight in compassion.

'I drank a gallon of black coffee in order to sober up fast, and then I broke every speed limit in the country driving up here——'

'Only to have me reject you because I was convinced I meant nothing to you.'

'Why the hell did you think that?' Niall's voice was raw.

'You were so determined that no one would know about us. You kept so much of your life separate—had your own flat——'

'Of course I did! You made it plain how much your privacy meant to you—and after the way you'd grown up I could see that for myself. Your cottage was your first private space—I couldn't invade that.'

'But I invited you!'

Even as she protested, she felt she knew what he was going to say.

'But you weren't ready for that, were you? Be honest, sweetheart—the first day we made love you were like a cat on hot bricks, terribly defensive about your home, edgy as hell because I was in your private haven.'

'I'd never done anything like that before——'

'I know——' his smile was infinitely gentle '—I *know*. And that was why I had to give you space, wait until you really wanted me——'

'But I did——' Saffron caught herself up sharply, remembering the way she'd felt at the time. 'You're right,' she admitted. 'I wanted to share my life with you, but I hadn't realised just what that meant in terms of giving up my privacy again.'

But Niall had. He had understood her better than she had herself, and had acted out of consideration for her feelings.

'And now?' he questioned softly.

'Niall—I love you more than life itself. I want to share my life with you—my hopes, my dreams, my body—and my home. If you really think you could exist in a doll's house.'

'If I was with you, anywhere would be a palace,' he assured her, in a voice that was husky with feeling.

One hand slid upwards to cup her cheek, drawing her face towards his for a kiss that was long and sweet and so tender that when he lifted his head again Saffron found that her cheeks were actually wet with tears of joy, tears she hadn't even been aware of having shed.

'I have to admit that I didn't just want to keep things quiet for your sake,' Niall told her. 'I needed time and peace in which to think about this feeling that had crept up on me so suddenly. I felt as if I'd been hit over the head by it—and I certainly didn't need the sort of hassle Owen Richards was likely to subject us to if he found out. And I'm sorry if I ruined things tonight. I should have kept it the way it was—kept it private——'

'No...' Saffron laid a gentle hand over his mouth to silence him. 'It was wonderful—magical.'

'Are you sure?'

'Positive.'

How could she not be sure? She might have worried about his desire to keep their affair secret, but how much more public could you get than tonight? How could she have any lingering doubts about a man who had wanted to display his love to the world?

'Perhaps this will convince you,' she whispered, pulling him towards her again, her arms lacing themselves around his neck, her lips soft and enticing.

'I'm convinced,' Niall sighed at last. 'But I may need to have that reinforced later.'

'Any time,' Saffron assured him lovingly. 'But now I think we'd better get back to the bonfire.'

'What the hell for?'

'I have a job to do.'

'Forget the food——'

'It's not the food.'

'Then, what——?'

'I have to find enough fireworks to spell out the word "YES" in letters five miles high.'

The glow that lit in his eyes was brighter than the blaze of the bonfire that could still be seen through the back window of the car.

'No need for fireworks,' he said when he had kissed her again. 'I'll take that as my answer.'

'But everyone from Kirkham will be wanting to know——'

'Damn everyone from Kirkham!' Niall declared dismissively. A moment later a wicked, teasing grin crossed his face. 'Anyway, don't you think that everyone will already have guessed what your answer was?'

His hands moved lower, sliding under the bright cotton of her sweatshirt and finding the soft warmth of her skin.

'What the hell do you think they suspect we've been up to all this time?'

The sensual touch of his hands, the look in those molten silver eyes, the thickness of his voice, told Saffron exactly what was in his mind, and excitement feathered across her skin, making her shiver in anticipation, her breathing quickening in time with the rapid beat of her heart.

'But Mr Forrester,' she teased softly, 'I thought you told me you were too old to make out in cars.'

'Too old?' he growled in her ear, pulling her close with a strength that communicated more of the way he was feeling than words ever could. 'Just try me——'

'Oh, I will...' she sighed, surrendering to an embrace that promised the sort of private firework display beside which the one still going on in the field behind them would pale into insignificance.

MILLS & BOON

CHRISTMAS CRACKERS

*A cracker of a gift pack full of
Mills & Boon goodies. You'll find...*

Passion—in *A Savage Betrayal* by Lynne Graham

A beautiful baby—in *A Baby for Christmas* by Anne McAllister

A Yuletide wedding—in *Yuletide Bride* by Mary Lyons

A Christmas reunion—in *Christmas Angel* by Shannon Waverly

Special Christmas price of 4 books
for £5.99 (usual price £7.96)

Published: November 1995

Christmas Journeys

4 new short romances all wrapped up in 1 sparkling volume.

Join four delightful couples as they journey home for the festive season—and discover the true meaning of Christmas...that love is the best gift of all!

A Man To Live For - Emma Richmond
Yule Tide - Catherine George
Mistletoe Kisses - Lynsey Stevens
Christmas Charade - Kay Gregory

Available: November 1995   **Price: £4.99**

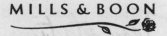

MILLS & BOON